Five from DRACO'S TAVERN

The Schumann Computer
When a wily chirpsithtra gets bartender Rick Schumann interested in the smartest computer in the galaxy, Schumann discovers his problems are only beginning . . .

Assimilating Our Culture, That's What They're Doing
There was a lot that even Schumann himself still had to learn about the glig—especially their taste in people . . .

Cruel and Unusual
One thing you could say about the chirpsithtra was that they sure knew how to make the punishment fit the crime . . .

The Subject is Closed
The chirpsithtra ruled the galaxy, were eons old, and knew all they wanted to know about life after death—at least that's what they told the first priest who'd ever come to Schumann's bar on the Moon . . .

Grammar Lesson
Never underestimate the power of possessive pronouns when you're a human dealing with an extraordinary chirpsithtra who has a special way with words . . .

Also by Larry Niven
published by Ballantine Books:

ALL THE MYRIAD WAYS

A GIFT FROM EARTH

THE FLIGHT OF THE HORSE

A HOLE IN SPACE

THE LONG *ARM* OF GIL HAMILTON

NEUTRON STAR

PROTECTOR

RINGWORLD

TALES OF KNOWN SPACE:
    The Universe of Larry Niven

WORLD OF PTAVVS

A WORLD OUT OF TIME

THE FLYING SORCERERS
    (with David Gerrold)

Convergent Series

Larry Niven

A Del Rey Book

BALLANTINE BOOKS • NEW YORK

Contents

Introduction

THIS book is my solution to a moral problem. If you've opened this book, you're already involved, and I suppose you'd better hear about it.

In 1969 I published a short-story collection, *The Shape of Space*. It was my second collection, my fourth book in five years of writing. The stories were a varied lot, ranging from vignette to novelet length and from hard science fiction to fantasy and mainstream.

Half the stories were set in a single consistent future. The Known Space timeline now covers a thousand years of the future, a huge volume of interstellar space, three collections, and four novels.

In 1975 I did something a lot of friends and strangers had been nagging me to do. I gathered together all of the Known Space stories and published most of them in *Tales of Known Space*. Two stories were left over, and I was writing a third. Those three science-fiction/detective stories became *The Long ARM of Gil Hamilton*, published in 1976.

Now, here's the problem. The first of the "Gil the Arm" stories, and many of the stories in *Tales of Known Space*, came out of *The Shape of Space*. About half the book.

In the meantime, I keep meeting people who started

reading my work during the past eight years, and have heard of *The Shape of Space,* and can't find it. The old paperback sells well at huckster tables during science-fiction conventions, when it can be found at all. It's easy to say that a reader can get half the stories by spending twice the money on two newer books. But what about "Convergent Series" and "The Deadlier Weapon"? People who never read them seem to know the plot lines; they get told around at parties.

I finally asked some people. Shall I gather up 30,000 words of new stories and put them in a book with 30,000 words of older stories from *The Shape of Space?* I was told to do it.

If you read *The Shape of Space* eight years ago . . . well, it's your money. You may regard this as a chance to see how my style and/or abilities have changed over the past ten years or so. I've added historical notes following some of the stories.

L.V.C.N.

Convergent
Series

Bordered in
Black

ONLY one figure stood in the airlock, though it was a cargo lock, easily big enough to hold both men. Lean and sandy haired, the tiny figure was obviously Carver Rappaport. A bushy beard now covered half his face. He waited patiently while the ramp was run up, and then he started down.

Turnbull, waiting at the bottom, suppressed growing uneasiness. Something was wrong. He'd known it the moment he heard that the *Overcee* was landing. The ship must have been in the solar system for hours. Why hadn't she called in?

And where was Wall Kameon?

Returning spacers usually sprinted down the ramp, eager to touch honest concrete again. Rappaport came down with slow, methodical speed. Seen close, his beard was ragged, unkempt. He reached bottom, and Turnbull saw that the square features were set like cement.

Rappaport brushed past him and kept walking.

Turnbull ran after him and fell into step, looking and feeling foolish. Rappaport was a good head taller, and where he was walking, Turnbull was almost running. He shouted above the background noise of the spaceport, "Rappaport, where's Kameon?"

Like Turnbull, Rappaport had to raise his voice. "Dead."

"Dead? Was it the ship? Rappaport, did the *ship* kill him?"

"No."

"Then what? Is his body aboard?"

"Turnbull, I don't want to talk about it. No, his body isn't aboard. His—" Rappaport ground the heels of his hands into his eyes, like a man with a blinding headache. "His grave," he said, emphasizing the word, "has a nice black border around it. Let's leave it at that."

But they couldn't, of course.

Two security officers caught up with them near the edge of the field. "Stop him," said Turnbull, and they each took an arm. Rappaport stopped walking and turned.

"Have you forgotten that I'm carrying a destruct capsule?"

"What about it?" For the moment Turnbull really didn't understand what he meant.

"Any more interference and I'll use it. Understand this, Turnbull. I don't care any more. Project Overcee is over. I don't know where I go from here. The best thing we can do is blow up that ship and stay in our own solar system."

"Man, have you gone crazy? What *happened* out there? You—meet aliens?"

"No comment.—No, I'll answer that one. We didn't meet aliens. Now tell your comedian friends to let go."

Turnbull let himself realize that the man wasn't bluffing. Rappaport was prepared to commit suicide. Turnbull, the instinctive politician, weighed changes and gambled.

"If you haven't decided to talk in twenty-four hours we'll let you go. I promise that. We'll keep you here 'til then, by force if necessary. Just to give you an opportunity to change your mind."

Rappaport thought it over. The security men still held his arms, but cautiously, now, standing as far back as they could, in case his personal bomb went off.

"Seems fair," he said at last, "if you're honest. Sure, I'll wait twenty-four hours."

"Good." Turnbull turned to lead the way back to his office. Instead, he merely stared.

The *Overcee* was red hot at the nose, glaring white at the tail. Mechs and techs were running in all directions. As Turnbull watched, the solar system's first faster-than-light spacecraft slumped and ran in a spreading, glowing pool.

. . . It had started a century ago, when the first ramrobots left the solar system. The interstellar ramscoop robots could make most of their journey at near light-speed, using a conical electromagnetic field two hundred miles across to scoop hydrogen fuel from interstellar space. But no man had ever ridden a ramrobot. None ever would. The ramscoop magnetic field did horrible things to chordate organisms.

Each ramrobot had been programmed to report back only if it found a habitable world near the star to which it had been assigned. Twenty-six had been sent out. Three had reported back—so far.

. . . It had started twelve years ago, when a well-known mathematician worked out a theoretical hyperspace over Einsteinian fourspace. He did it in his spare time. He considered the hyperspace a toy, an example of pure mathematics. And when has pure mathematics been anything but good clean fun?

. . . It had started ten years ago, when Ergstrom's brother Carl demonstrated the experimental reality of Ergstrom's toy universe. Within a month the UN had financed Project Overcee, put Winston Turnbull in charge, and set up a school for faster-than-light astronauts. The vast number of applicants was winnowed to ten "hypernauts." Two were Belters; all were experienced spacers. The training began in earnest. It lasted eight years, while Project Overcee built the ship.

. . . It had started a year and a month ago, when

two men climbed into the almost luxurious lifesystem of the *Overcee,* ran the ship out to Neptune's orbit under escort, and vanished.

One was back.

Now his face was no stonier than Turnbull's. Turnbull had just watched his work of the last ten years melt and run like quicksilver. He was mad clean through; but his mind worked furiously. Part of him, the smaller part, was wondering how he would explain the loss of ten billion dollars worth of ship. The rest was reviewing everything it could remember about Carver Geoffrey Rappaport and William (Wall) Kameon.

Turnbull entered his office and went straight to the bookshelf, sure that Rappaport was following. He pulled out a leather-bound volume, did something to the binding and poured two paper cups full of amber fluid. The fluid was bourbon, and it was more than ice cold.

Rappaport had seen this bookcase before, yet he wore a faintly puzzled frown as he took a cup. He said, "I didn't think I'd ever anticipate anything again."

"The bourbon?"

Rappaport didn't answer. His first swallow was a gulp.

"Did you destroy your ship?"

"Yes. I set the controls so it would only melt. I didn't want anyone hurt."

"Commendable. And the overcee motor? You left it in orbit?"

"I hard-landed it on the Moon. It's gone."

"That's great. Just great. Carver, that ship cost ten billion dollars to build. We can duplicate it for four, I think, because we won't be making any false starts, but you—"

"Hell you wouldn't." Rappaport swirled the bourbon in his cup, looking down into the miniature whirlpool. He was twenty to thirty pounds lighter than he had been a year ago. "You build another *Overcee* and you'll be making one enormous false start. We were wrong, Turnbull. It's not our universe. There's nothing out there for us."

"It *is* our universe." Turnbull let the quiet certainty show in his politician's voice. He needed to start an argument—he needed to get this man to talking. But the certainty was real, and always had been. It was humanity's universe, ready for the taking.

Over the rim of his cup Rappaport looked at him in exasperated pity. "Turnbull, can't you take my word for it? It's not our universe, and it's not worth having anyway. What's out there is—" He clamped his mouth shut and turned away in the visitor's chair.

Turnbull waited ten seconds to point up the silence. Then he asked, "Did you kill Kameon?"

"Kill Wall? You're out of your mind!"

"Could you have saved him?"

Rappaport froze in the act of turning around. "No," he said. And again, "No. I tried to get him moving, but he wouldn't—stop it! Stop needling me. I can walk out anytime, and you couldn't stop me."

"It's too late. You've aroused my curiosity. What about Kameon's black-bordered grave?"

No answer.

"Rappaport, you seem to think that the UN will just take your word and dismantle Project Overcee. There's not a prayer of that. Probability zero. In the last century we've spent tens of billions of dollars on the ram-robots and the *Overcee,* and now we can rebuild her for four. The only way to stop that is to tell the UN exactly why they shouldn't."

Rappaport didn't answer, and Turnbull didn't speak again. He watched Rappaport's cigarette burning unheeded in the ashtray, leaving a strip of charred wet paper. It was uncharacteristic of the former Carver Rappaport to forget burning cigarettes, or to wear an untrimmed beard and sloppily cut hair. The man had been always clean shaven; that man had lined up his shoes at night, every night, even when staggering drunk.

Could he have killed Kameon for being sloppy?

—and then turned messy himself as he lost his self-respect? Stranger things had happened in the days when it took eight months to reach Mars. —No, Rappaport had not done murder. Turnbull would have bet high on that. And Kameon would have won any fair fight. Newspapermen had nicknamed him The Wall when he was playing guard for the Berlin Nazis.

"You're right. Where do I start?"

Turnbull was jerked out of his abstraction. "Start at the beginning. When you went into hyperspace."

"We had no trouble there. Except with the windows. You shouldn't have put windows on the *Overcee.*"

"Why not? What did you see?"

"Nothing."

"Well, then?"

"You ever try to find your blind spot? You put two dots on a piece of paper, maybe an inch apart, and you close one eye, focus on one dot and slowly bring the paper up to your face. At some point the other dot disappears. Looking at the window in overcee is like your blind spot expanding to a two-foot square with rounded corners."

"I assume you covered them up."

"Sure. Would you believe it, we had trouble finding those windows? When you wanted them they were invisible. We got them covered with blankets. Then every so often we'd catch each other looking under the blankets. It bothered Wall worse than me. We could have made the trip in five months instead of six, but we had to keep coming out for a look around."

"Just to be sure the universe was still there."

"Right."

"But you did reach Sirius."

"Yes. We reached Sirius . . ."

Ramrobot #6 had reported from Sirius B, half a century ago. The Sirius stars are an unlikely place to look for habitable worlds, since both stars are blue-white giants. Still, the ramrobots had been programmed to test for excessive ultraviolet. Sirius B was worth a look.

The ship came out where Sirius was two bright stars. It turned its sharp nose toward the dimmer star and remained motionless for twenty minutes, a silver torpedo shape in a great, ungainly cradle studded with heavy electromagnetic motors. Then it was gone again.

Now Sirius B was a searing ball of light. The ship began to swing about, like a hound sniffing the breeze, but slowly, ponderously.

"We found four planets," said Rappaport. "Maybe there were more, but we didn't look. Number Four was the one we wanted. It was a cloudy ball about twice the size of Mars, with no moon. We waited until we'd found it before we started celebrating."

"Champagne?"

"Hah! Cigars and drunk pills. And Wall shaved off his grubby beard. My God, we were glad to be out in space again! Near the end it seemed like those blind spots were growing around the edges of the blankets. We smoked our cigars and sucked our drunk pills and yakked about the broads we'd known. Not that we hadn't done *that* before. Then we slept it off and went back to work . . ."

The cloud cover was nearly unbroken. Rappaport moved the telescope a bit at a time, trying to find a break. He found several, but none big enough to show him anything. "I'll try infrared," he said.

"Just get us down," Wall said irritably. He was always irritable lately. "I want to get to work."

"And I want to be sure we've got a place to land."

Carv's job was the ship. He was pilot, astrogator, repairman, and everything but the cook. Wall was the cook. Wall was also the geologist, astrophysicist, biologist, and chemist—the expert on habitable planets, in theory. Each man had been trained nine years for his job, and each had some training as backup man for the other; and in each case the training had been based largely on guesswork.

The picture on the scope screen changed from a featureless disk to a patterned ball as Carv switched to infrared. "Now which is water?" he wondered.

"The water's brighter on the night side, and darker on the day side. See?" Wall was looking over his shoulder. "Looks like about forty percent land. Carv, those clouds might cut out enough of the ultraviolet to let people live in what gets through."

"Who'd want to? You couldn't see the stars." Carv turned a knob to raise the magnification.

"Hold it right there, Carv. Look at that. There's a white line around the edge of that continent."

"Dried salt?"

"No. It's warmer than what's around it. And it's just as bright on the night side as on the day."

"I'll get us a closer look."

The *Overcee* was in orbit, three hundred miles up. By now the continent with the "hot" border was almost entirely in shadow. Of the three supercontinents, only one showed a white shoreline under infrared.

Wall hung at the window, looking down. To Rappaport he looked like a great ape. "Can we do a reentry glide?"

"In this ship? The *Overcee* would come apart like a cheap meteor. We'll have to brake to a full stop above the atmosphere. Want to strap down?"

Kameon did, and Carv watched him do it before he went ahead and dropped the overcee motor. *I'll be glad to be out of here,* he thought. *it's getting so Wall and I hate the sight of each other.* The casual, uncaring way Kameon fastened his straps jarred his teeth. He knew that Kameon thought he was finicky to the point of psychasthenia.

The fusion drive started and built up to one gee. Carv swung the ship around. Only the night side showed below, with the faint blue light of Sirius A shining softly off the cloud cover. Then the edge of dawn came up in torn blue-white cloud. Carv saw an enormous rift in the cloud bank and turned ship to shift their path over it.

Mountains and valleys, and a wide river . . . Patches of wispy cloud shot by, obscuring the view, but they could see down. Suddenly there was a black line, a twisting ribbon of India ink, and beyond that the ocean.

Only for a moment the ocean showed, and then the rift jogged east and was gone. But the ocean was an emerald green.

Wall's voice was soft with awe. "Carv, there's life in that water."

"You sure?"

"No. It could be copper salts or something. Carv, we've got to get *down* there!"

"Oh, wait your turn. Did you notice that your hot border is black in visible light?"

"Yah. But I can't explain it. Would it be worth our while to turn back after you get the ship slowed?"

Carv fingered his neatly trimmed Vandyke. "It'd be night over the whole continent before we got back there. Let's spend a few hours looking at that green ocean."

The *Overcee* went down on her tail, slowly, like a cautious crab. Layer after layer of cloud swallowed her without trace, and darkness fell as she dropped. The key to this world was the word "moonless." Sirius B-IV had had no oversized moon to strip away most of her atmosphere. Her air pressure would be comfortable at sea level, but only because the planet was too small to hold more air. That same low gravity produced a more gentle pressure gradient, so that the atmosphere reached three times as high as on Earth. There were cloud layers from ground to 130 kilometers up.

The *Overcee* touched down on a wide beach on the western shore of the smallest continent. Wall came out first, then Carv lowered a metal oblong as large as himself and followed it down. They wore lightly pressurized vac suits. Carv did nothing for twenty minutes while Wall opened the box out flat and set the carefully packed instruments into their grooves and notches. Finally Wall signaled, in an emphatic manner. By taking off his helmet.

Carv waited a few seconds, then followed suit.

Wall asked, "Were you waiting to see if I dropped dead?"

"Better you than me." Carv sniffed the breeze. The air was cool and humid, but thin. "Smells good enough. No. No, it doesn't. It smells like something rotting."

"Then I'm right. There's life here. Let's get down to the beach."

The sky looked like a raging thunderstorm, with occasional vivid blue flashes that might have been lightning. They were flashes of sunlight penetrating tier upon tier of cloud. In that varying light Carv and Wall stripped off their suits and went down to look at the ocean, walking with shuffling steps in the light gravity.

The ocean was thick with algae. Algae were a bubbly green blanket on the water, a blanket that rose and fell like breathing as the insignificant waves ran beneath. The smell of rotting vegetation was no stronger here than it had been a quarter of a mile back. Perhaps the smell pervaded the whole planet. The shore was a mixture of sand and green scum so rich that you could have planted crops in it.

"Time I got to work," said Wall. "You want to fetch and carry for me?"

"Later maybe. Right now I've got a better idea. Let's get the hell out of each other's sight for an hour."

"That *is* brilliant. But take a weapon."

"To fight off maddened algae?"

"Take a weapon."

Carv was back at the end of an hour. The scenery had been deadly monotonous. There was water below a green blanket of scum six inches deep; there was loamy sand, and beyond that dry sand; and behind the beach were white cliffs, smoothed as if by countless rainfalls. He had found no target for his laser cutter.

Wall looked up from a binocular microscope, and grinned when he saw his pilot. He tossed a depleted pack of cigarettes. "And don't worry about the air plant!" he called cheerfully.

Carv came up beside him. "What news?"

"It's algae. I can't name the breed, but there's not much difference between this and any terrestrial algae, except that this sample is all one species."

"That's unusual?" Carv was looking around him in wonder. He was seeing a new side to Wall. Aboard ship Wall was sloppy almost to the point of being dangerous, at least in the eyes of a Belter like Carv. But now he was at work. His small tools were set in neat rows on portable tables. Bulkier instruments with legs were on flat rock, the legs carefully adjusted to leave their platforms exactly horizontal. Wall handled the binocular microscope as if it might dissolve at a touch.

"It is," said Wall. "No little animalcules moving among the strands. No variations in structure. I took samples from depths up to six feet. All I could find was the one algae. But otherwise—I even tested for proteins and sugars. You could eat it. We came all this way to find pond scum."

They came down on an island five hundred miles south. This time Carv helped with the collecting. They got through faster that way, but they kept getting in each other's way. Six months spent in two small rooms had roused tempers too often. It would take more than a few hours on ground before they could bump elbows without a fight.

Again Carv watched Wall go through his routines. He stood just within voice range, about fifty yards away, because it felt so good to have so much room. The care Wall exercised with his equipment still amazed him. How could he reconcile it with Wall's ragged fingernails and his thirty hours growth of beard?

Well, Wall was a flatlander. All his life he'd had a whole planet to mess up, and not a crowded pressure dome or the cabin of a ship. No flat ever learned real neatness.

"Same breed," Wall called.

"Did you test for radiation?"

"No. Why?"

"This thick air must screen out a lot of gamma rays. That means your algae can't mutate without local radiation from the ground."

"Carv, it had to mutate to get to its present form. How could all its cousins just have died out?"

"That's your field."

A little later Wall said, "I can't get a respectable background reading anywhere. You were right, but it doesn't explain anything."

"Shall we go somewhere else?"

"Yah."

They set down in deep ocean, and when the ship stopped bobbing Carv went out the airlock with a glass bucket. "Its a foot thick out there," he reported. "No place for a Disneyland. I don't think I'd want to settle here."

Wall sighed his agreement. The green scum lapped thickly at the *Overcee*'s gleaming metal hull, two yards below the sill of the airlock.

"A lot of planets must be like this," said Carv. "Habitable, but who needs it?"

"And I wanted to be the first man to found an interstellar colony."

"And get your name in the newstapes, the history books—"

"—And my unforgettable face on every trivis in the solar system. Tell me, shipmate, if you hate publicity so much, why have you been trimming that Vandyke so prettily?"

"Guilty. I like being famous. Just not as much as you do."

"Cheer up then. We may yet get all the hero worship we can stand. This may be something bigger than a new colony."

"What could be bigger than that?"

"Set us down on land and I'll tell you."

On a chunk of rock just big enough to be called an island, Wall set up his equipment for the last time. He was testing for food content again, using samples from Carv's bucket of deep ocean algae.

Carv stood by, a comfortable distance away, watching the weird variations in the clouds. The very highest were moving across the sky at enormous speeds, swirling and changing shape by the minutes and seconds. The noonday light was subdued and early. No doubt about it, Sirius B-IV had a magnificent sky.

"Okay, I'm ready." Wall stood up and stretched. "This stuff isn't just edible. I'd guess it would taste as good as the food supplements they were using on Earth before the fertility laws cut the population down to something reasonable. I'm going to taste it now."

The last sentence hit Carv like an electric shock. He was running before it was quite finished, but long before he could get there his crazy partner had put a dollup of green scum in his mouth, chewed and swallowed. "Good," he said.

"You—utter—damned—fool."

"Not so. I knew it was safe. The stuff had an almost cheesy flavor. You could get tired of it fast, I think, but that's true of anything."

"Just *what* are you trying to *prove?*"

"That this alga was tailored as a food plant by biological engineers. Carv, I think we've landed on somebody's private farm."

Carv sat heavily down on a rainwashed white rock. "Better spell that out," he said, and heard that his voice was hoarse.

"I was going to. Suppose there was a civilization that had cheap, fast interstellar travel. Most of the habitable planets they found would be sterile, wouldn't they? I mean, life is an unlikely sort of accident."

"We don't have the vaguest idea how likely it is."

"All right, pass that. Say somebody finds this planet, Sirius B-IV, and decides it would make a nice farm planet. It isn't good for much else, mainly because of the variance in lighting, but if you dropped a specially bred food alga in the ocean, you'd have a dandy little farm. In ten years there'd be oceans of algae, free for the carting. Later, if they *did* decide to colonize, they could haul the stuff inland and use it for fertilizer. Best of all, it wouldn't mutate. Not here."

Carv shook his head to clear it. "You've been in space too long."

"Carv, the plant looks *bred*—like a pink grapefruit. And where did all its cousins go? Now I can tell you. They got poured out of the breeding vat because they weren't good enough."

Low waves rolled in from the sea, low and broad beneath their blanket of cheesy green scum. "All right," said Carv. "How can we disprove it?"

Wall looked startled. *"Dis*prove it? Why would we want to do that?"

"Forget the glory for a minute. If you're right, we're trespassing on somebody's property without knowing anything about the owner—except that he's got dirt-cheap interstellar travel, which would make him a tough enemy. We're also introducing our body bacteria onto his pure edible algae culture. And how would we explain, if he suddenly showed up?"

"I hadn't thought of it that way."

"We ought to cut and run right now. It's not as if the planet was worth anything."

"No. No, we can't do that."

"Why not?"

The answer gleamed in Wall's eyes.

Turnbull, listening behind his desk with his chin resting in one hand. interrupted for the first time in minutes. "A good question. I'd have gotten out right then."

"Not if you'd just spent six months in a two-room cell with the end of everything creeping around the blankets."

"I see." Turnbull's hand moved almost imperceptibly, writing, *NO WINDOWS IN OVERCEE #2! Oversized viewscreen?*

"It hadn't hit me that hard. I think I'd have taken off if I'd have been sure Wall was right, and if I could have talked him into it. But I couldn't, of course. Just the thought of going home then was enough to set Wall shaking. I thought I might have to knock him on the head when it came time to leave. We had some hibernation drugs aboard, just in case."

He stopped. As usual, Turnbull waited him out.

"But then I'd have been all alone." Rappaport finished his drink, his second, and got up to pour a third. The bourbon didn't seem to affect him. "So we stood there on that rocky beach, both of us afraid to leave and both afraid to stay . . ."

Abruptly Wall got up and started putting his tools away. "We can't disprove it, but we can prove it easily enough. The owners must have left artifacts around. If we find one, we run. I promise."

"There's a big area to search. If we had any sense we'd run now."

"Will you drop that? All we've got to do is find the ramrobot probe. If there's anyone watching this place they must have seen it come down. We'll find footprints all over it."

"And if there aren't any footprints? Does that make the whole planet clean?"

Wall closed his case with a snap. Then he stood, motionless, looking very surprised. "I just thought of something," he said.

"Oh, not again."

"No, this is for real, Carv. The owners must have left a long time ago."

"Why?"

"It must be thousands of years since there were

enough algae here to use as a food supply. We should have seen ships taking off and landing as we came in. They'd have started their colony too, if they were going to. Now it's gone beyond that. The planet isn't fit for anything to live on, with the soupy oceans and the smell of things rotting."

"No."

"Dammit, it makes sense!"

"It's thin. It sounds thin even to me, and I *want* to believe it. Also, it's too pat. It's just too close to the best possible solution we could dream up. You want to bet our lives on it?"

Wall hoisted his case and moved toward the ship. He looked like a human tank, moving in a stormy darkness lit by shifting, glaring beams of blue light. Abruptly he said, "There's one more point. That black border. It has to be contaminated algae. Maybe a land-living mutant, that's why it hasn't spread across the oceans. It would have been cleaned away if the owners were still interested."

"All *right*. Hoist that thing up and let's get inside."

"Hmph?"

"You've finally said something we can check. The eastern shore must be in daylight by now. Let's get aboard."

At the border of space they hovered, and the Sun burned small and blinding white at the horizon. To the side Sirius A was a tiny dot of intense brilliance. Below, where gaps in the cloud cover penetrated all the way to the surface, a hair-thin black line ran along the twisting beach of Sirius B-IV's largest continent. The silver thread of a major river exploded into a forking delta, and the delta was a black triangle shot with lines of silvery green.

"Going to use the scope?"

Carv shook his head. "We'll see it close in a few minutes."

"You're in quite a hurry, Carv."

"You bet. According to you, if that black stuff is

some form of life, then this farm's been deserted for thousands of years at least. If it isn't, then what is it? It's too regular to be a natural formation. Maybe it's a conveyor belt."

"That's right. Calm me down. Reassure me."

"If it is, we go up fast and run all the way home." Carv pulled a lever and the ship dropped from under them. They fell fast. Speaking with only half his attention, Carv went on. "We've met just one other sentient race, and they had nothing like hands and no mechanical culture. I'm not complaining, mind you. A world wouldn't be fit to live in without dolphins for company. But why should we get lucky twice? We don't want to meet the farmer, Wall."

The clouds closed over the ship. She dropped more slowly with every kilometer. Ten kilometers up she was almost hovering. Now the coast was spread below them. The black border was graded: black as night on Pluto along the sea, shading off to the color of the white sand and rocks along the landward side.

Wall said, "Maybe the tides carry the dead algae inland. They'd decay there. No, that won't work. No moon. Nothing but solar tides."

They were a kilometer up. And lower. And lower.

The black was moving, flowing like tar, away from the drive's fusion flame.

Rappaport had been talking down into his cup, his words coming harsh and forced, his eyes refusing to meet Turnbull's. Now he raised them. There was something challenging in that gaze.

Turnbull understood. "You want me to guess? I won't. What was the black stuff?"

"I don't know if I want to prepare you or not. Wall and I, we weren't ready. Why should you be?"

"All right, Carver, go ahead and shock me."

"It was people."

Turnbull merely stared.

"We were almost down when they started to scatter from the downblast. Until then it was just a dark field, but when they started to scatter we could see moving specks, like ants. We sheered off and landed on the water offshore. We could see them from there."

"Carver, when you say people, do you mean—people? Human?"

"Yes. Human. Of course they didn't act much like it . . ."

A hundred yards offshore, the *Overcee* floated nose up. Even seen from the airlock, the natives were obviously human. The telescope screen brought more detail.

They were no terrestrial race. Nine feet tall, men and women both, with wavy black hair growing from the eyebrows back to halfway down the spine, hanging almost to the knees. Their skins were dark, as dark as the darkest Negro, but they had chisel noses and long heads and small, thin-lipped mouths.

They paid no attention to the ship. They stood or sat or lay where they were, men and women and children jammed literally shoulder to shoulder. Most of the seaside population was grouped in large rings with men on the outside and women and children protected inside.

"All around the continent," said Wall.

Carv could no more have answered than he could have taken his eyes off the scope screen.

Every few minutes there was a seething in the mass as some group that was too far back pulled forward to reach the shore, the food supply. The mass pushed back. On the fringes of the circles there were bloody fights, slow fights in which there were apparently no rules at all.

"How?" said Carv. "How?"

Wall said, "Maybe a ship crashed. Maybe there was a caretaker's family here, and nobody ever came to pick them up. They must be the farmer's children, Carv."

"How long have they been here?"

"Thousands of years at least. Maybe tens or hundreds of thousands." Wall turned his empty eyes away from the screen. He swiveled his couch so he was looking at the back wall of the cabin. His dreary words flowed out into the cabin.

"Picture it, Carv. Nothing in the world but an ocean of algae and a few people. Then a few hundred people, then hundreds of thousands. They'd never have been allowed near here unless they'd had the bacteria cleaned out of them to keep the algae from being contaminated. Nothing to make tools out of, nothing but rock and bone. No way of smelting ores, because they wouldn't even have fire. There's nothing to *burn*. They had no diseases, no contraceptives, and no recreation but breeding. The population would have exploded like a bomb. Because nobody would starve to death, Carv. For thousands of years nobody would starve on Sirius B-IV."

"They're starving now."

"Some of them. The ones that can't reach the shore." Wall turned back to the scope screen. "One continual war," he said after awhile. "I'll bet their height comes from natural selection."

Carv hadn't moved for a long time. He had noticed that there were always a few men inside each protective circle, and that there were always men outside going inside and men inside going outside. Breeding more people to guard each circle. More people for Sirius B-IV.

The shore was a seething blackness. In infrared light it would have shown brightly, at a temperature of 98.6° Fahrenheit.

"Let's go home," said Wall.

"Okay."

"And did you?"

"No."

"In God's name, why not?"

"We *couldn't*. We had to see it all, Turnbull. I don't

understand it, but we did, both of us. So I took the ship up and dropped it a kilometer inshore, and we got out and started walking toward the sea.

"Right away, we started finding skeletons. Some were clean. A lot of them looked like Egyptian mummies, skeletons with black dried skin stretched tight over the bones. Always there was a continuous low rustle of—well, I guess it was conversation. From the beach. I don't know what they could have had to talk about.

"The skeletons got thicker as we went along. Some of them had daggers of splintered bone. One had a chipped stone fist ax. You see, Turnbull, they were intelligent. They could make tools, if they could find anything to make tools out of.

"After we'd been walking awhile we saw that some of the skeletons were alive. Dying and drying under that overcast blue sky. I'd thought that sky was pretty once. Now it was—horrible. You could see a shifting blue beam spear down on the sand and sweep across it like a spotlight until it picked out a mummy. Sometimes the mummy would turn over and cover its eyes.

"Wall's face was livid, like a dead man's. I knew it wasn't just the light. We'd been walking about five minutes, and the dead and living skeletons were all around us. The live ones all stared at us, apathetically, but still staring, as if we were the only things in the world worth looking at. If they had anything to wonder with, they must have been wondering what it was that could move and still not be human. We couldn't have looked human to them. We had shoes and coveralls on, and we were too small.

"Wall said, 'I've been wondering about the clean skeletons. There shouldn't be any decay bacteria here.'

"I didn't answer. I was thinking how much this looked like a combination of Hell and Belsen. The only thing that might have made it tolerable was the surrealistic blue lighting. We couldn't really believe what we were seeing.

" 'There weren't enough fats in the algae,' said Wall. 'There was enough of everything else, but no fats.'

"We were closer to the beach now. And some of the mummies were beginning to stir. I watched a pair behind a dune who looked like they were trying to kill each other, and then suddenly I realized what Wall had said.

"I took his arm and turned to go back. Some of the long skeletons were trying to get up. I knew what they were thinking. *There may be meat in those limp coverings. Wet meat, with water in it. There just may.* I pulled at Wall and started to run.

"He couldn't run. He tried to pull loose. I had to leave him. They couldn't catch me, they were too starved, and I was jumping like a grasshopper. But they got Wall, all right. I heard his destruct capsule go off. Just a muffled pop."

"So you came home."

"Uh huh." Rappaport looked up like a man waking from a nightmare. "It took seven months. All alone."

"Any idea why Wall killed himself?"

"You crazy? He didn't want to get *eaten.*"

"Then why wouldn't he run?"

"It wasn't that he wanted to kill himself, Turnbull. He just decided it wasn't worthwhile saving himself. Another six months in the *Overcee,* with the blind spots pulling at his eyes and that nightmare of a world constantly on his mind—it wasn't worth it."

"I'll bet the *Overcee* was a pigpen before you blew it up."

Rappaport flushed. "What's that to you?"

"You didn't think it was worthwhile either. When a Belter stops being neat it's because he wants to die. A dirty ship is deadly The air plant gets fouled. Things float around loose, ready to knock your brains out when the drive goes on. You forget where you put the meteor patches—"

"All right. I made it, didn't I?"

"And now you think we should give up space."

Rappaport's voice went squeaky with emotion. "Turnbull, aren't you convinced *yet?* We've got a paradise here, and you want to leave it for—that. Why? Why?"

"To build other paradises, maybe. Ours didn't happen by accident. Our ancestors did it all, starting with not much more than what was on Sirius B-IV."

"They had a *hell*uva lot more." A faint slurring told that the bourbon was finally getting to Rappaport.

"Maybe they did at that. But now there's a better reason. These people you left on the beach. They need our help. And with a new *Overcee,* we can give it to them. What do they need most, Carver? Trees or meat animals?"

"Animals." Rappaport shuddered and drank.

"Well, that could be argued. But pass it. First we'll have to make soil." Turnbull leaned back in his chair, face upturned, talking half to himself. "Algae mixed with crushed rock. Bacteria to break the rock down. Earthworms. Then grass . . ."

"Got it all planned out, do you? And you'll talk the UN into it, too. Turnbull, you're good. But you've missed something."

"Better tell me now then."

Rappaport got carefully to his feet. He came over to the desk, just a little unsteadily, and leaned on it so that he stared down into Turnbull's eyes from a foot away. "You've been assuming that those people on the beach really were the farmer's race. That Sirius B-IV has been deserted for a long, long time. But what if some kind of carnivore seeded that planet? Then what? The algae wouldn't be for them. They'd let the algae grow, plant food animals, then go away until the animals were jammed shoulder to shoulder along the coast. Food animals! You understand, Turnbull?"

"Yes. I hadn't thought of that. And they'd breed them for *size* . . ."

The room was deadly quiet.

"Well?"

"Well, we'll simply have to take that chance, won't we?"

————————

Bordered in Black does not belong to the Known Space universe. (And if that statement means nothing to you, don't worry about it.)

When I wrote *Bordered in Black,* Known Space had not taken form. I was playing with some preliminary ideas, and one of these—the "Blind Spot" effect of this form of faster-than-light travel—was later incorporated into Known Space. But it's a different timeline entirely.

Similar statements hold for *One Face,* which follows. Hair styles and human colony worlds from this story later entered Known Space; but the story does not belong to that universe.

A further note to both stories. Many astronomers believed for a time (the time following our discovery that Venus's atmosphere was sixty times as thick as Earth's, and hotter than Hell) that an Earth-sized world could not have an Earthlike atmosphere unless there was an oversized moon to skim away most of the more normal "Venusian" atmosphere. That idea has now been discredited.

One
Face

AN alarm rang: a rising, falling crescendo, a mechanical shriek of panic. The baritone voice of the ship's Brain blared, "Strac Astrophysics is not in his cabin! Strac Astrophysics, report to your cabin immediately! The *Hogan's Goat* will Jump in sixty seconds."

Verd sat bolt upright, then forced himself to lie down again. The *Hogan's Goat* had not lost a passenger through carelessness in all the nearly two centuries of Verd's captaincy. Passengers were *supposed* to be careless. If Strac didn't reach his room Verd would have to postpone Jump to save his life: a serious breach of custom.

Above the green coffin which was his Jump couch the Brain said, "Strac Astrophysics is in his cabin and protected."

Verd relaxed.

"Five," said the Brain. "Four. Three . . ."

In various parts of the ship, twenty-eight bodies jerked like springs released "Oof," came a complaint from the Jump couch next to Verd's. "That felt strange. Dam' strange."

"Um," said Verd.

Lourdi Coursefinder tumbled out of her Jump couch. She was a blend of many subdivisions of man, bearing the delicate, willowy beauty born of low-

gravity worlds She was Verd's wife, and an experienced traveler. Now she looked puzzled and disturbed.
"Jump never felt like that. What do you suppose—?"

Verd grunted as he climbed out. He was a few pounds overweight. His face was beefy, smooth and unlined, fashionably hairless. So was his scalp, except for a narrow strip of black brush which ran straight up from between his brow ridges and continued across his scalp and downward until it faded out near the small of his back. Most of the hair had been surgically implanted. Neither wrinkled skin nor width of hair strip could number a man's years, and superficially Verd might have been anywhere from twenty to four hundred years old. It was in his economy of movement that his age showed. He did things the easy way, the fast way. He never needed more than seconds to find it, and he always took that time. The centuries had taught him well.

"I don't know," he said. "Let's find out what it was. Brain!" he snapped at a wall speaker.

The silence stretched like a nerve.

"Brain?"

One wall arced over to become the ceiling, another jogged inward to leave room for a piece of the total conversion drive, a third was all controls and indicators for the ship's Brain. This was the crew common room. It was big and comfortable, a good place to relax, and no crewman minded its odd shape. Flat ceilings were for passengers.

Verd Spacercaptain, Lourdi Coursefinder, and Parliss Lifesystems sat along one wall, watching the fourth member of the crew.

Chanda Metalminds was a tall, plain woman whose major beauty was her wavy black hair. A strip three inches wide down the center of her scalp had been allowed to grow until it hung to the region of her coccyx. Satin black and satin smooth, it gleamed and rippled as she moved. She stood before the biggest of the Brain screens, which now showed a diagram of the *Hogan's Goat,* and she used her finger as a pointer.

"The rock hit here." Chanda's finger rested almost halfway back along the spinal maze of lines and little black squares which represented the Jumper section. The *Hogan's Goat* was a sculptured torpedo, and the Jumper machinery was its rounded nose and its thick spine and its trailing wasplike sting. You could see it in the diagram. The rest of the *Goat* had been designed to fit the Jumper. And the Jumper was cut by a slanting line, bright red, next to Chanda's fingertip.

"It was a chunk of dirty ice, a typical piece of comet head," said Chanda. "The meteor gun never had a chance at it. It was too close for that when we came out of overspace. Impact turned the intruder to plasma in the Jumper. The plasma cone knocked some secondary bits of metal loose, and they penetrated *here.* That rained droplets of high-speed molten metal all through the ship's Brain."

Parliss whistled. He was tall, ash blond, and very young. "That'll soften her up," he murmured irreverently. He winced under Chanda's glare and added, "Sorry."

Chanda held the glare a moment before she continued. "There's no chance of repairing the Brain ourselves. There are too many points of injury, and most of them too small to find. Fortunately the Brain can still solve problems and obey orders. Our worst problem seems to be this motor aphasia. The Brain can't speak, not in any language. I've circumvented that by instructing the Brain to use Winsel code. Since I don't know the extent of the damage precisely, I recommend we land the passengers by tug instead of trying to land the *Goat.*"

Verd cringed at the thought of what the tug captains would say. "Is that necessary?"

"Yes, Verd. I don't even know how long the Brain will answer to Winsel code. It was one of the first things I tried. I didn't really expect it to work, and I doubt it would on a human patient."

"Thanx, Chanda." Verd stood up and the Brain surgeon sat down. "All I have to say, group, is that we're going to take a bad loss this trip. The Brain is sure to need expensive repairs, and the Jumper will have to be almost completely torn out. It gave one awful discharge when the meteor hit, and a lot of parts are fused— Lourdi, what's wrong? We can afford it."

Lourdi's face was bloodless. Her delicate surgeon's fingers strangled the arms of her chair.

"Come on," Verd said gently. What could have driven her into such a panic? "We land on Earth and take a vacation while the orbital repair companies do the worrying. What's wrong with that?"

Lourdi gave her head a spastic shake. "We can't do that. Oh, Eye of Kdapt, I didn't dare believe it. Verd, we've got to fix the Jumper out here."

"Not a chance. But—"

"Then we've got trouble," Lourdi had calmed a little, but it was the calm of defeat. "I couldn't ask the Brain to do it, so I used the telescope myself. That's not Sol."

The others looked at her.

"It's not the Sun. It's a greenish-white dwarf, a dead star. I couldn't find the Sun."

Once it had its orders, the Brain was much faster with the telescope than Lourdi. It confirmed her description of the star which was where Sol should have been, and added that it was no star in the Brain's catalogue. Furthermore the Brain could not recognize the volume of space around it. It was still scanning stars, hoping to find its bearings.

"But the rock hit *after* we came out of overspace. *After!*" Verd said between his teeth. "How could we have gone anywhere else?" Nobody was listening.

They sat in the crew common room drinking droobleberry juice and vodka.

"We'll have to tell the passengers something," said Chanda. Nobody answered, though she was dead right. Interstellar law gave any citizen free access to a computer. In space the appropriate computer was a ship's Brain. By now the passengers must have discovered that the Brain was incommunicado.

Lourdi stopped using her glass to make rings on the tabletop. "Chanda, will you translate for me?"

Chanda looked up. "Of course."

"Ask the Brain to find the planet in this system which most resembles Saturn."

"Saturn?" Chanda's homely face lost its hopeful expression. Nonetheless she began tapping on the rim of a Brain speaker with the end of a stylus, tapping in the rhythms of Winsel code.

Almost immediately a line of short and long white dashes began moving left to right across the top of the Brain screen. The screen itself went white, cleared, showed what looked like a picture of Saturn. But the ring showed too many gaps, too well defined. Chanda said, "Fifth major planet from primary. Six moons. Period: 29.46 years. Distance from Sun: 9.45 A.U. Diameter: 72,018 miles. Type: gas giant. So?"

Lourdi nodded. Verd and Parliss were watching her intently. "Ask it to show us the second and third planets."

The second planet was in its quarter phase. The Brain screen showed it looking like a large moon, but less badly pocked, and with a major difference: the intensely bright area across the middle. Chanda translated the marching dots: "Distance: 1.18 A.U. Period: 401.4. Diameter: 7918 miles. No moons. No air."

The third planet— "That's Mars," said Lourdi.

It was.

And the second planet was Earth.

"I believe I know what has happened." Verd was almost shouting. Twenty-seven faces looked back at him across the dining room. He was addressing crew and passengers, and he had to face them in person, for the Brain could no longer repeat his words over the stateroom speakers.

"You know that a Jumper creates an overspace in

which the speed of light becomes infinite in the neighborhood of the ship. When—"

"Almost infinite," said a passenger.

"That's a popular misconception," Verd snapped. He found that he did not like public speaking, not under these conditions. With an effort he resumed his speaking voice. "The speed of light goes all the way to infinity. Our speed is kept finite by the braking spine, which projects out of the effective neighborhood. Otherwise we'd go simultaneous: we'd be everywhere at once along a great circle of the universe. The braking spine is that thing like a long stinger that points out behind the ship.

"Well, there was a piece of ice in our way, inside the range of our meteor gun, when we came out of overspace. It went through the Jumper and into the Brain.

"The damage to the Brain is secondary. Something happened to the Jumper while the meteor was in there. Maybe some metal vaporized and caused a short circuit. Anyway the *Goat* Jumped back into the counterpart of overspace." Verd stopped. Was he talking over their heads? "You understand that when we say we travel in an overspace of Einsteinian space, we really mean a *subspace* of that overspace?"

A score of blank faces looked back at him. Doggedly Verd went on. "We went into the counterpart of that subspace. The speed of light went to zero."

A murmur of whispering rose and fell. Nobody laughed.

"The braking spine stuck out, or we'd have been in there until the bitter end of time. Well, then. In a region around the ship, the speed of light was zero. Our mass was infinite, our clocks and hearts stopped, the ship became an infinitely thin disk. This state lasted for no time in ship's time, but when it ended several billion years had passed."

A universal gasp, then pandemonium. Verd had expected it. He waited it out.

"Billion?" "Kdapt stomp it—" "Oh my God." "Practical joke, Marna. I must say—" "Shut up and let him finish!"

The shouting died away. A last voice shouted, "But if our mass was infinite—"

"Only in a region around the ship!"

"Oh," said a dark stick figure Verd recognized as Strac Astrophysics. Visibly he shrugged off a vision of suns and galaxies snatched brutally down upon his cringing head by the *Goat*'s infinite gravity.

"The zero effect has been used before," Verd continued in the relative quiet. "For suspended animation, for very long-range time capsules, et cetera. To my knowledge it has never happened to a spacecraft. Our position is very bad. The Sun has become a greenish-white dwarf. The Earth has lost all its air and has become a one-face world; it turns one side forever to the Sun. Mercury isn't there anymore. Neither is the Moon.

"You can forget the idea of going home, and say good-bye to anyone you knew outside this ship. This is the universe, ourselves and nobody else, and our only duty is to survive. We will keep you informed of developments. Anyone who wishes his passage money refunded is welcome to it."

In a crackle of weak graveyard laughter, Verd bobbed his head in dismissal.

The passengers weren't taking the hint. Hearing the captain in person was as unique to them as it was to Verd. They sat looking at each other, and a few got up, changed their minds, and sat down again. One called, "What will you do next?"

"Ask the Brain for suggestions," said Verd. "Out, now!"

"We'd like to stay and listen," said the same man. He was short and broad and big footed, probably from one of the heavier planets, and he had the rough-edged compactness of a land tank. "We've the legal right to consult the Brain at any time. If it takes a translator we should have a translator."

Verd nodded. "That's true." Without further comment he turned to Chanda and said, "Ask the Brain what actions will maximize our chance of survival for maximal time."

Chanda tapped her stylus rhythmically against the rim of the Brain speaker.

The dining area was raucous with the sound of breathing and the stealthy shuffling of feet. Everyone seemed to be leaning forward.

The Brain answered in swiftly moving dots of light. Chanda said, "Immediately replace—Eye of Kdapt!" Chanda looked very startled, then grinned around at Verd. "Sorry, Captain. 'Immediately replace Verd Spacercaptain with Strac Astrophysics in supreme command over *Hogan's Goat.*' "

In the confusion that followed, Verd's voice was easily the loudest. "Everybody out! Everybody but Strac Astrophysics."

Miraculously, he was obeyed.

Strac was a long, tall oldster, old in habits and manners and mode of dress. A streak of black-enameled steel wool emphasized his chocolate scalp, and his ears spread like wings. Once Verd had wondered why Strac didn't have them fixed. Later he had stopped wondering. Strac obviously made a fetish of keeping what he was born with. His hairline began not between his eyes, but at the very top of his forehead, and it petered out on his neck. His fingernails grew naturally. They must have needed constant trimming.

He sat facing the members of the crew, waiting without impatience.

"I believe you've traveled on my ship before," said Verd. "Have you ever said or done anything to give the Brain, or any passenger, the idea that you might want to command the *Hogan's Goat?*"

"Certainly not!" Strac seemed as ruffled by the suggestion as Verd himself. "The Brain must be insane," he muttered venomously. Then his own words backlashed him, and in fear he asked, "*Could* the Brain be insane?"

"No," Chanda answered. "Brains of this type can

be damaged, they can be destroyed, but if they come up with an answer it's the right one. There's a built-in doubt factor. Any ambiguity gives you an Insufficient Data."

"Then why would it try to take my command?"

"I don't know. Captain, there's something I should tell you."

"What's that?"

"The Brain has stopped answering questions. There seems to be some progressive deterioration going on. It stopped even before the passengers left. If I give it orders in Winsel it obeys, but it won't answer back."

"Oh, Kdapt take the Brain!" Verd rubbed his temples with his fingertips. "Parliss, what did the Brain know about Strac?"

"Same as any other passenger. Name, profession, medical state and history, mass, world of origin. That's all."

"Hmph. Strac, where were you born?"

"The Canyon," said Strac. "Is that germane?"

"I don't know. Canyon is a lonely place to grow up, I imagine."

"It is, in a way. Three hundred thousand is a tiny population for a solar system, but there's no room for more. Above the Canyon rim the air's too thin to breathe. I got out as soon as I could. Haven't been back in nearly a century."

"I see."

"Captain, I doubt that. In the Canyon there's no lack of company. It's the culture that's lonely. Everybody thinks just like everybody else. You'd say there's no cultural cross-fertilization. The pressure to conform is brutal."

"Interesting," said Verd, but his tone dismissed the subject. "Strac, do you have any bright ideas that the Brain might have latched onto somehow? Or do you perhaps have a reputation so large in scientific circles that the Brain might know of it?"

"I'm sure that's not the case."

"Well, do you have any ideas at all? We need them badly."

"I'm afraid not. Captain, just what is our position? It seems that everyone is dead but us. How do we cope with an emergency like that?"

"We don't," said Verd. "Not without time travel, and that's impossible. It is, isn't it?"

"Of course."

"Chanda, exactly what did you ask the Brain? How did you phrase it?"

"Maximize the probability of our surviving for maximum time. That's what you asked for. Excuse me, Captain, but the Brain almost certainly assumed that 'maximum time' meant forever."

"All right. Parliss, how long will the ship keep us going?"

Parliss was only thirty years old, and burdened with youth's habitual unsureness; but he knew his profession well enough. "A long time, Captain. Decades, maybe centuries. There's some boosterspice seeds in our consignment for the Zoo of Earth; if we could grow boosterspice aboard ship we could keep ourselves young. The air plant will work as long as there's sunlight or starlight. But the food converter—well, it can't *make* elements, and eventually they'll get lost somewhere in the circuit, and we'll start getting deficiency diseases, and—hmmm. I could probably keep us alive for a century and a half, and if we institute cannibalism we could—"

"Never mind. Let's call that our limit if we stay in space. We've got other choices, Strac, none of them pleasant.

"We can get to any planet in the solar system using the matter-conversion drive. We've enough solid chemical fuel in the landing rockets to land us on any world the size of Venus or smaller. With the matter-conversion drive we can take off from anywhere, but the photon beam would leave boiling rock behind us. We can do all that, but there's no point to it, because nothing in the solar system is habitable."

"If I may interrupt," said Strac. "Why do we have a matter-conversion drive?"

"Excuse me?"

"The *Hogan's Goat* has the Jumper to move between worlds, and the solids to land and take off. Why does such a ship need another reaction drive? Is the Jumper so imprecise?"

"Oh. No, that's not it. You see, the math of Jumper travel postulates a figure for the mass of a very large neighborhood, a neighborhood that takes in most of the local group of galaxies. That figure is almost twice the actual rest mass in the neighborhood. So we have to accelerate until the external universe is heavy enough for us to use the Jumper."

"I see."

"Even with total mass conversion we have to carry a tremendous mass of fuel. We use neutronium; anything less massive would take up too much room. Then, without the artificial gravity to protect us it would take over a year to reach the right velocity. The drive gives us a good one hundred gee in uncluttered space." Verd grinned at Strac's awed expression. "We don't advertise that. Passengers might start wondering what would happen if the artificial gravity went off.

"Where was I? . . . Third choice: we can go on to other stars. Each trip would take decades, but by refueling in each system we could reach a few nearby stars in the hundred and fifty years Parliss gives us. But every world we ever used must be dead by now, and the G-type stars we can reach in the time we've got may have no useful worlds. It would be a gamble."

Strac shifted uneasily. "It certainly would. We don't necessarily need a G-type sun, we can settle under any star that won't roast us with ultraviolet, but habitable planets are rare enough. Can't you order the Brain to search out a habitable planet and go there?"

"No," said Lourdi, from across the room. "The telescope isn't that good, not when it has to peer out of one gravity well into another. The light gets all bent up."

"And finally," said Verd, "if we did land on an

Earth-sized planet that looked habitable, and then
found out it wasn't, we wouldn't have the fuel to land
anywhere else. Well, what do you think?"

Strac appeared to consider. "I think I'll go have a
drink. I think I'll have several. I wish you'd kept our
little predicament secret a few centuries longer." He
rose with dignity and turned to the door, then spoiled
the exit by turning back. "By the way, Captain, have
you ever been to a one-face world? Or have your trav-
els been confined to the habitable worlds?"

"I've been to the Earth's Moon, but that's all. Why?"

"I'm not sure," said Strac, and he left looking
thoughtful. Verd noticed that he turned right. The bar
was aft of the dining room, to the left.

Gloom settled over the dining area. Verd fumbled
in his belt pouch, brought forth a white tube not much
bigger than a cigarette. Eyes fixed morosely on a wall,
he hung the tube between his lips, sucked through it,
inhaled at the side of his mouth. He exhaled cool, thick
orange smoke.

The muscles around his eyes lost a little of their
tension.

Chanda spoke up. "Captain, I've been wondering
why the Brain didn't answer me directly, why it didn't
just give us a set of detailed instructions."

"Me too. Have you got an answer?"

"It must have computed just how much time it had
before its motor aphasia became complete. So instead
of trying to give a string of detailed instructions it
would never finish, it just named the person most likely
to have the right answer. It gave us what it could in the
few seconds it had left."

"But why Strac? Why not me, or one of you?"

"I don't know," Chanda said wearily. The damage
to the Brain had hit her hard. Not surprising; she had
always treated the Brain like a beloved but retarded
child. She closed her eyes and began to recite, "Name,
profession, mass, world of origin, medical history.
Strac, astrophysics, the Canyon . . ."

In the next few days, each member of the crew was busy at his own specialty.

Lourdi Coursefinder spent most of her time at the telescope. It was a powerful instrument, and she had the Brain's limited help. But the worlds of even the nearest stars were only circular dots. The sky was thick with black suns, visible only in the infrared. She did manage to find Earth's Moon—more battered than ever, in a Trojan orbit, trailing sixty degrees behind the parent planet in her path around the Sun.

Parliss Lifesystems spent his waking hours in the ship's library, looking up tomes on the medical aspects of privation. Gradually he was putting together a detailed program that would keep the passengers healthy for a good long time, and alive for a long time after that, with safety factors allowing for breakdown of the more delicate components of the life-support system. Later he planned to prepare a similar program using cannibalism to its best medical advantage. That part would be tricky, involving subtle psychological effects from moral shock.

Slowly and painfully, with miniature extensible waldos, Chanda searched out the tiny burns in the Brain's cortex and scraped away the charred semiconducting ash. "Probably won't help much," she admitted grimly, "but the ash may be causing short circuits. It can't *hurt* to get it out. I wish I had some fine wire."

Once he was convinced that the Jumper was stone-cold dead, Verd left it alone. That gave him little to do but worry. He worried about the damage to the Brain, and wondered if Chanda was being overoptimistic. Like a surgeon forced to operate on a sick friend, she refused even to consider that the Brain might get worse instead of better. Verd worried, and he checked the wiring in the manual override systems for the various drives, moving along outside the hull in a vac suit.

He was startled by the sight of the braking spine. Its ultrahard metal was as shiny as ever, but it was two-thirds gone. Sublimation, over several billion years.

He worried about the passengers too. Without the constant entertainment provided by the Brain, they would be facing the shock of their disaster virtually unaided. The log had a list of passengers, and Chanda got the Brain to put it on the screen, but Verd could find few useful professions among them.

Strac Astrophysics

Jimm Farmer

Avran Zooman

The other professions were all useless here. Taxer, Carmaker, Adman—he was lucky to find anything at all. "All the same," he told Lourdi one night, "I'd give anything to find a Jak FTLsystems aboard."

"How 'bout a Harlan Alltrades?"

"On this tub? Specializing nonspecialists ride the luxury liners." He twisted restlessly in the air between the sleeping plates. "Wanta buy an aircar? It was owned by a sniveling coward—"

Jimm Farmer was the heavy-planet man, with long, smooth muscles and big broad feet. His Jinxian accent implied that he could probably kick holes in hullmetal. "I've never worked without machinery," he said. "Farming takes an awful lot of machinery. Diggers, plowers, seeders, transplanters, aerators, you name it. Even if you gave me seeds and a world to grow them on, I couldn't do anything by myself." He scratched his bushy eyebrows. For some reason he'd let them grow outward from the end of his hairline, like the crossbar on an upside-down T. "But if all the passengers and crew pitched in and followed directions, and if they didn't mind working like robots, I think we could raise something, if we had a planet with good dirt and some seeds."

"At least we've got the seeds," said Verd. "Thanx, Mr. Farmer."

Verd had first seen Avran Zooman walking through the hall at the beginning of the trip. Zooman was a shocking sight. His thin strip of hair was bleached-bone white and started halfway back on his scalp. His skin had faint lines in it, like the preliminary grooves in tooled leather. Verd had avoided him until now. Obviously the man belonged to one of those strange, nearly extinct religious orders which prohibit the taking of boosterspice.

But he didn't behave like a religious nut. Verd found him friendly, alert, helpful, and likable. His thick We Made It accent was heavy with stressed esses.

"In this one respect we are lucky," Avran was saying. "Or you are lucky. I should have been lucky enough to miss my ship. I came to protect your cargo, which is a selection of fertile plant seeds and frozen animal eggs for the Zoo of Earth Authority."

"Exactly what's in the consignment?"

"Nearly everything you could think of, Captain. The Central Government wished to establish a zoo to show all the life that Earth has lost as a result of her intense population compression. I suspect they wished to encourage emigration. This is the first consignment, and it contains samples of every variety of nondomestic life on We Made It. There were to be other shipments from other worlds, including some expensive mutations from Wunderland designed to imitate the long extinct 'big cats.' We do not have those, nor the useless decorative plants such as orchids and cactus, but we do have everything we need for farming."

"Have you got an incubator for the animals?"

"Unfortunately not. Perhaps I could show you how to make one out of other machinery." Avran smiled humorously. "But there is a problem. I am fatally allergic to boosterspice extract. Thus I will be dead in less than a century, which unfortunately limits the length of any journey that I can make."

Verd felt his face go numb. He was no more afraid of death than the next man, but—frantically he tried to sort his climbing emotions before they strangled him. Admiration, wonder, shame, horror, fear. How could Avran live so casually with death? How could he have reached such a state of emotional maturity in what could be no more than fifty years? Shame won out, shame at his own reaction, and Verd felt himself flushing.

Avran looked concerned. "Perhaps I should come back later," he suggested.

"No! I'm all right." Verd had found his tabac stick without thinking. He pulled in a deep, cooling draft of orange smoke, and held it in his lungs for a long moment.

"A few more questions," he said briskly. "Does the Zoo consignment have grass seed? Are there any bacteria or algae?"

"Grass, yes. Forty-three varieties. No bacteria, I'm afraid."

"That's not good. It takes bacteria to turn rock dust into fertile soil."

"Yes." Avran considered. "We could start the process with sewage from the ship mixed with intestinal flora. Then add the rock dust. We have earthworms. It might work."

"Good."

"Now I have a question, Captain. What is that?"

Verd followed his pointing finger. "Never seen a tabac stick?"

Avran shook his head.

"There's a funny tranquilizer in tobacco that helps you concentrate, lets you block out distractions. People used to have to inhale tobacco smoke to get it. That caused lung cancer. Now we do it better. Are there tobacco plants in the consignment?"

"I'm afraid not. Can you give up the habit?"

"If I have to. But I'll hate it."

Verd sat for a moment after Avran had left, then got up and hunted down Parliss. "Avran claims to be allergic to boosterspice. I want to know if it's true. Can you find out?"

"Sure, Captain. It'll be in the medical record."

"Good."

"Why would he lie, Captain?"

"He may have a religious ban on boosterspice. If so,

he might think I'd shoot him full of it just because I need him. And he'd be right."

There was no point in interviewing Strac Astrophysics again. Parliss told him that Strac spent most of his time in his room, and that he had found a pocket computer somewhere.

"He must have something in mind," said Parliss.

The next day Parliss came to the cabin. "I've gone through the medical histories," he said. "We're all in good shape, except Avran Zooman and Laspia Waitress. Avran told the truth. He's allergic to boosterspice. Laspia has a pair of cultured arms, no telling how she lost the old ones, and both ulnas have machinery in them. One's a dooper, one's a multirange sonic. I wonder what that sweet girl is doing armed to the teeth like that."

"So do I. Can you sabotage her?"

"I put an extension-recharger in her room. If she tries to shoot anyone she'll find her batteries are drained."

The sixth day was the day of mutiny.

Verd and Parliss were in the crew common room, going over Parliss' hundred-and-fifty-year schedule for shipboard living, when the door opened to admit Chanda. The first hint came from Chanda's taut, determined expression. Then Verd saw that someone had followed her in. He stood up to protest, then stood speechless as a line of passengers trooped into the crew common room, filling it nearly to bursting.

"I'm sorry, Captain," said Chanda. "We've come to demand your resignation."

Verd, still standing, let his eyes run over them. The pretty auburn-haired woman in front, the one who held her arms in an inconspicuously strained attitude—she must be Laspia Waitress. Jimm Farmer was also in the front rank. And Strac Astrophysics, looking acutely embarrassed. Many looked embarrassed, and many looked angry; Verd wasn't sure what they were angry

at, or who. He gave himself a few seconds to think.
Let 'em wait it out . . .

"On what grounds?" he asked mildly.

"On the ground that it's the best chance we have to
stay alive," said Chanda.

"That's not sufficient grounds. You know that. You
need a criminal charge to bring against me: dereliction
of duty, sloppiness with the drive beam, murder, vio-
lation of religious tenets, drug addiction. Do you wish
to make such a charge?"

"Captain, you're talking about impeachment—legal
grounds for mutiny. We don't have such grounds. We
don't want to impeach you, regardless."

"Well, just what did you think this was, Chanda?
An election?"

"We're inviting you to resign."

"Thanx, but I think not."

"We could impeach you, you know." Jimm Farmer
was neither angry nor embarrassed; merely interested.
"We could charge you with addiction to tabac sticks,
try you, and convict you."

"*Tabac sticks?*"

"Sure, everybody knows they're not addictive. The
point is that you can't find a higher court to reverse
our decision."

"I guess that's true. Very well, go ahead."

Parliss broke in, in a harsh whisper. "Chanda, what
are you *doing?*" His face, scalp, and ears burned sunset red.

The tall woman said, "Quiet, Parl. We're only doing
what needs to be done."

"You're crazy with grief over that damn mechanical
moron."

Chanda flashed him a smoking glare. Parliss returned it. She turned away, aloofly ignoring him.

Strac spoke for the first time. "Don't make us use
force, Captain."

"Why not? Do you idiots realize what you're asking?" Verd's control was going. He'd been a young
man when the *Hogan's Goat* was built. In nearly two

centuries he'd flown her further than the total distance to Andromeda; nursed her and worried about her and lived his life in her lighted, rushing womb. What he felt must have showed in his face, for the girl with the auburn hair raised her left arm and held it innocently bent, pointed right at him. Probably it was the sonic; no doubt he would have been swathed in calming vibrations if her batteries had worked. But all he felt was nausea and a growing rage.

"I do," Strac said quietly. "We're asking you to make it possible for us to give you back your ship after this is over."

Verd jumped at him. A cold corner of his mind was amazed at himself, but most of him only wanted to get his hands around Strac's bony, fragile throat. He glimpsed Laspia Waitress staring in panic at her forearms, and then a steel hand closed around his ankle and *jerked*. Verd stopped in midair.

It was Jimm Farmer. He had jumped across the room like a kangaroo. Verd looked back over his shoulder and carefully kicked him under the jaw. Jimm looked surprised and hurt. He squeezed!

"All right!" Verd yelped. More softly, "All right. I'll resign."

The autodoc mended two cracked ankle bones, injected mysterious substances into the badly bruised lower terminal of his Achilles tendon, and ordered a week of bed rest.

Strac's plans were compatible. He had ordered the ship to Earth. Since the *Goat* was still moving at nearly lightspeed, and had gone well past the solar system, the trip would take about two weeks.

Verd began to enjoy himself. For the first time since the last disastrous Jump, he was able to stop worrying for more than minutes at a time. The pressure was off. The responsibility was no longer his. He even persuaded Lourdi to cooperate with Strac. At first she would have nothing to do with the mutineers, but Verd convinced her that the passengers depended on her. Professional pride was a powerful argument.

After a week on his back Verd started moving around the ship, trying to get an idea of the state of the ship's morale. He did little else. He was perversely determined not to interfere with the new captain.

Once Laspia Waitress stopped him in the hall. "Captain, I've decided to take you into my confidence. I am an ARM, a member of the Central Government Police of Earth. There's a badly wanted man aboard this ship." And before Verd could try to humor her out of it she had produced authentic-looking credentials.

"He's involved in the Free Wunderland conspiracy," she went on. "Yes, it still exists. We had reason to believe he was aboard the *Hogan's Goat,* but I wasn't sure of it until he found some way to disarm me. I still haven't identified him yet. He could be anyone, even—"

"Easy, easy," Verd soothed her. "I did that. I didn't want anyone wandering around my ship with concealed weapons."

Her voice cracked. "You fool! How am I going to arrest him?"

"Why should you? Who would you turn him over to if you did? What harm can he do now?"

"What *harm?* He's a revolutionary, a—a seditionist!"

"Sure. He's fanatically determined to free Wunderland from the tyranny of the Central Government of Earth. But Wunderland and the Central Government have been dead for ages, and we haven't a single Earthman on board. Unless you're one."

He left her sputtering helplessly.

When he thought about it later it didn't seem so funny. Many of the passengers must be clinging to such an outmoded cause, unwilling to face the present reality. When that defense gave out, he could expect cases of insanity.

Surprisingly, Straç had talked to nobody, except to ask questions of the crew members. If he had plans they were all his own. Perhaps he wanted one last look at Earth, ancient grandmother Earth, dead now of old age. Many passengers felt the same.

Verd did not. He and Lourdi had last seen Earth twelve years ago—subjective time—when the *Goat* was getting her life-support systems rejuvenated. They had spent a wonderful two months in Rio de Janeiro, a hive of multicolored human beings moving among buildings that reached like frustrated spacecraft toward the sky. Once they had even seen two firemanes, natives of l'Elephant, shouldering their way unconcerned among the bigger humans, but shying like fawns at the sight of a swooping car. Perhaps firemanes still lived somewhere in the smoky arms of this galaxy or another. Perhaps even humans lived, though they must be changed beyond recognition. But Verd did not want to look on the corpse face of Earth. He preferred to keep his memories unspoiled.

He was not asked.

On the tenth day the *Goat* made turnover. Verd thought of the drive beam sweeping its arc across deserted asteroidal cities. Neutronium converted to a destroying blast of pure light. In civilized space a simple turnover required seconds of calculation on the part of the Brain, just to keep the drive beam pointed safely. Anything that light touched would vanish. But now there was nothing to protect.

On the fifteenth ship's-day morning the Earth was a wide, brilliant crescent, blinding bright where the seas had dried across her sunward face. The Sun shone with eerie greenish-white radiance beyond the polarized windows. Verd and Lourdi were finishing breakfast when Strac appeared outside the one-way transparent door. Lourdi let him in.

"I thought I'd better come personally," said Strac. "I've called for a meeting in the crew common room in an hour. I'd appreciate it if you'd be there, Verd."

"I'd just as soon not," said Verd. "Thanx anyway. Have a roast dove?"

Strac politely declined, and left. He had not repeated his invitation.

"He wasn't just being polite," Lourdi told him. "He needs you."

"Let 'im suffer."

Lourdi took him gently by the ears and turned him to face her—a trick she had developed to get his undivided attention. "Friend, this is the wrong time to play prima donna. You talked me into serving the usurper on grounds that the passengers needed my skills. I'm telling you they need yours."

"Dammit, Lourdi, if they needed me I'd still be captain!"

"They need you as a crewman!"

Verd set his jaw and looked stubborn. Lourdi let go, patted his ears gently, and stepped back. "That's my say. Think it through, Lord and Master."

Six people circled the table. Verd was there, and Lourdi and Parliss and Chanda. Strac occupied the captain's chair, beneath the Brain screen. The sixth man was Jimm Farmer.

"I know what we have to do now," said Strac. His natural dignity had deepened lately, though his shoulders sagged as if ship's gravity were too much for him, and his thin, dark face had lost the ability to smile. "But I want to consider alternatives first. To that end I want you all to hear the answers to questions I've been asking you individually. Lourdi, will you tell us about the Sun?"

Lourdi stood up. She seemed to know exactly what was wanted.

"It's very old," she said. "Terribly old and almost dead. After our Jumper went funny the Sun seems to have followed the main sequence all the way. For awhile it got hotter and brighter and bigger, until it blew up into a red giant. That's probably when Mercury disappeared. Absorbed.

"Sol could have left the main sequence then, by going nova for example, but if it had there wouldn't be any inner planets. So it stayed a red giant until there wasn't enough fuel to burn to maintain the pressure, and then the structure collapsed.

"The Sun contracted to a white dwarf. What with unradiated heat working its way out, and heat of contraction, and fusion reactions still going on inside, it continued to give off light, and still does, even though for all practical purposes there's no fuel left. You can't burn iron. So now the Sun's a greenish dwarf, and in a few million years it'll be a black one."

"Only millions?"

"Yes, Strac. Only millions."

"How much radiation is being put out now?"

Lourdi considered. "About the same as in our time, but it's bluer light. The Sun is much hotter 'han we knew it, but all its light has to radiate through a smaller surface area. Do you want figures?"

"No thanx, Lourdi. Jimm Farmer, could you grow foodstuffs under such a star?"

Peculiar question, thought Verd. He sat up straighter, fighting a horrible suspicion.

Jimm looked puzzled, but answered readily. "If the air was right and I had enough water, sure I could. Plants like ultraviolet. The animals might need protection from sunburn."

Strac nodded. "Lourdi, what's the state of the galaxy?"

"Lousy," she said promptly. "Too many dead stars, and most of what's left are blue-white and white giants. Too hot. I'll bet that any planet in this neighborhood that has the right temperature for life will be a gas giant. The young stars are all in the tips of the galactic arms, and they've been scattered by the spin of the galaxy. We can find *some* young stars in the globular clusters. Do you want to hear about them?"

"We'd never reach them," said Verd. His suspicion was a certainty. He blew orange smoke and waited, silently daring Strac to put his intention into words.

"Right," said Strac. "Chanda, how is the Brain?"

"Very, very sick. It might stop working before the

decade's end. It'll never last out the century, crippled as it is." Chanda wasn't looking so good herself. Her eyes were red, underlined with blue shadows. Verd thought she had lost mass. Her hair hadn't had its usual care. She continued, as if to herself, "Twice I've given it ordinary commands and gotten the Insufficient Data sign. That's very bad. It means the Brain is starting to distrust the data in its own memory banks."

"Just how bad *is* that?"

"It's a one-way street, with a wiped mind at the end. There's no way to stop it."

"Thanx, Chanda." Strac was carrying it off, but beneath his battered dignity he looked determined and—frightened. Verd thought he had reason. "Now you know everything," he told them. "Any comments?"

Parliss said, "If we're going star hunting we should stop on Pluto and shovel up an air reserve. It'd give us a few decades leeway."

"Uh huh. Anything else?"

Nobody answered.

"Well, that's that." Strac drew a deep breath, let it out slowly. "There's too much risk in searching the nearby stars. We'll have to make do with what we've got. Chanda, please order the Brain to set us down on the highest flat point in Earth's noon-equator region."

Chanda didn't move. Nobody moved.

"I knew it," Verd said, very quietly. His voice echoed in the greater quiet. The crew common room was like a museum exhibit. Everyone seemed afraid to move. Everyone but Jimm Farmer, who in careful silence was getting to his feet.

"Didn't you understand, Strac?" Verd paused and tried to make his voice persuasive. "The Brain put you in charge because you had more useful knowledge than the rest of us. You were supposed to find a new home for the human race."

They were all staring at Strac with varying degrees of horror. All but Jimm, who stood patiently waiting for the others to make up their minds.

"You were not supposed to give up and take us home to die!" Verd snapped. But Strac was ignoring him. Strac was glaring at them all in rage and contempt.

Parliss, normally Nordic-pale, was white as moonlight. "Strac, it's dead! Leave it! We can find another world—"

"You mewling litter of blind idiots."

Even Jimm Farmer looked shocked.

"Do you think I'd kill us all for a twinge of homesickness? Verd, you know better than that, even if nobody else does. They were on *your* back, twenty-seven adults and all their potential children, all waiting for you to tell them how to die. Then came the mutiny. Now you're free! They've all shifted to *my* back!"

His eyes left Verd's and ranged over his shocked, silent crew. "Idiots blindly taking orders from a damaged mechanical brain. Believing everything you're told. Lourdi!" he snapped. "What does 'one face' mean?"

Lourdi jumped. "It means the body doesn't rotate with respect to its primary."

"It doesn't mean the planet has only one face?"

"Wha-at?"

"The Earth has a back side to it."

"Sure!"

"What does it look like?"

"I don't know." Lourdi thought a moment. "The Brain knows. You remember you asked Chanda to make the Brain use the radar to check the back side. Then she couldn't get the Brain to show us the picture. We can't use the telescope because there's no light, not even infrared. It must be terribly cold. Colder than Pluto."

"You don't know," said Strac. "But I do. We're going down. Chanda?"

"Tell us about it," said Jimm Farmer.

"No," said Verd.

He had not known that he was going to speak. He

had known only that they had given Strac the responsibility without the power to match it. But Strac felt the responsibility; he carried it in his bent shoulders and bleak expression, in his deep, painful breathing, in his previous attempts to pass the buck to someone else. Why would Strac want to land on Earth? Verd didn't know. But Strac must know what he was doing. Otherwise he couldn't have moved at all!

Someone had to back him up.

"No." Verd spoke with all the authority he could muster. "Chanda, take her down."

"Tell us about it," Jimm repeated. The authority backing his flat, menacing tone was his own titanic physical strength.

"No. Shut up, Jimm. Or we'll let you make all the decisions from now on."

Jimm Farmer thought it over, suddenly laughed and sat down. Chanda picked up her stylus and began tapping on the speaker.

The *Hogan's Goat* lay on her side, nearly in the center of a wide, ancient asteroid crater. There, marring the rounded spine with its long stinger, was the ragged, heat-stained hole that marked a meteor strike. There, along two-thirds of the length of her belly, was the gash a rock had made in the last seconds of the landing. And at the tail, forward of the braking spine, that static explosion of curved metal strips was where the photon drive had been torn free.

A small, fiercely bright Sun burned down from a black sky.

It had been a bad landing. Even at the start the Brain was a fraction of a second slow in adjusting ship's gravity, so that the floor had bucked queasily under them as they dropped. Then, when they were already falling toward the crater, Strac had suddenly added a new order. The photon drive had to be accessible after landing. Chanda had started tapping— and the ship had flipped on its side.

The *Hogan's Goat* had never been built to land on its side. Many of the passengers sported bruises. Avran Zooman had broken an arm. Without booster-spice the bone would be slow to heal.

A week of grinding labor was nearly over.

Only servomachinery now moved on the crater floor. From Verd's viewpoint most of the activity seemed to center around a gigantic silver tube which was aimed like a cannon at a point ten degrees above the horizon. The drive tube had been towed up against the crater wall, and a mountain of piled, heat-fused earth now buried its lower end. Cables and fuel pipes joined it higher up.

"Hi! Is that you, Captain?"

Verd winced. "I'm on top of the crater wall," he said, because Strac couldn't locate him from the sound of his voice. The indeterminate voice had to be Strac. Only Strac would bellow into a suit radio. "And I'm not the captain."

Strac floated down beside him. "I thought I'd see the sights."

"Good. Have a seat."

"I find it strange to have to call you Verd," said the astrophysicist. "It used to be just 'Captain.' "

"Serves you right for staging a mutiny—Captain."

"I always knew my thirst for power would get me in trouble."

They watched as a tractor-mounted robot discon-nected a fuel pipe from the drive, then rolled back. A moment later a wash of smoky flame burst from the pipe. The flame changed color and intensity a dozen times within a few seconds, then died as abruptly as it had begun. The robot waited for the white heat to leave the pipe, then rolled forward to reconnect it.

Verd asked, "Why are you so calm all of a sudden?"

"My job's over," Strac said with a shrug in his voice. "Now it's in the lap of Kdapt."

"Aren't you taking an awful chance?"

"Oh? You've guessed what I'm trying to do?"

"I hope it wasn't a secret. There's only one thing you could be doing, with the photon drive all laid out and braced like that. You're trying to spin the Earth."

"Why?" Strac baited him.

"You must be hoping there's air and water frozen on the dark side. But it seems like a thin chance. Why were you afraid to explain?"

"You put it that way, then ask why I didn't put it to a vote? Verd, would you have done what I did?"

"No. It's too risky."

"Suppose I tell you that I *know* the air and water is there. It has to be there. I can tell you what it looks like. It's a great shallow cap of ice, stratified out according to freezing points, with water ice on the bottom, then carbon dioxide, all the way up through a thick nitrogen layer to a few shifting pools of liquid helium. Surely you don't expect a one-face world to have a gaseous atmosphere? It would all freeze out on the night side. It has to!"

"It's there? There's air there? Your professional word?"

"My word as an astrophysicist. There's frozen gas back there."

Verd stretched like a great cat. He couldn't help himself. He could actually feel the muscles around his eyes and cheeks rippling as they relaxed, and a great grin crawled toward his ears. "You comedian!" he laughed. "Why didn't you say so?"

"Suppose I kept talking?"

Verd turned to look at him.

"You'll have thought of some of these things yourself. Can we breathe that air? Billions of years have passed. Maybe the composition of the air changed before it froze. Maybe too much of it boiled off into space while the sun was a red giant. Maybe there's too much, generated by outgasing after the Moon was too far away to skim it off. Lourdi said the Sun is putting out about the right amount of heat, but just how close will it be to a livable temperature? Can Jimm Farmer make us topsoil? There'll be live soil on the nightside, possibly containing frozen live bacteria, but can we get there if we have to?

"Worst of all, can we spin the Earth in the first place? I know the drive's strong enough. I don't know about the Earth. There can't be any radioactivity left in the Earth's core, so the planet should be solid rock all the way to the center. But solid rock flows under pressure. We'll get earthquakes. Kdapt only knows how bad. Well, Captain, would you have taken all those risks?"

"She blows."

The drive was on.

Traces of hydrogen, too thin to stop a meteor, glowed faintly in the destroying light. A beam like a spotlight beam reached out over the sharp horizon, pointing dead east. Anything that light touched would flame and blow away on the wings of a photon wind. The drive nosed a little deeper into its tomb of lava.

The ground trembled. Verd turned on his flying unit, and Strac rose after him. Together they hovered over the quivering Earth. Other silver specks floated above the plain.

In space the drive would be generating over a hundred savage gravities. Here . . . almost none. Almost.

Little quick ripples came running in from the eastern horizon. They ran across the crater floor in parallel lines of dancing dust, coming closer and closer together. Rocks showered down from the old ringwall.

"Maybe I wouldn't have risked it," said Verd. "I don't know."

"That's why the Brain put me in charge. Did you see the oxygen ice as we went by the night side? Or was it too dark? To you this frozen atmosphere is pure imagination, isn't it?"

"I'll take your professional word."

"But I don't need to. I *know* it's there."

Lines of dust danced over the shaking ground. But the ripples were less violent, and were coming less frequently.

"The Brain was damaged," Verd said softly.

"Yes," said Strac, frowning down into the old crater. Suddenly he touched his controls and dropped. "Come on, Verd. In a few days there'll be air. We've got to be ready for wind and rain."

Like Banquo's
Ghost

ON a hot, lovely fall day I drove out to Stardrive Laboratories. If all went well, that was the day the *Snarkhunter #3* probe would send its final message from Alpha Centauri. The *Times* had assigned me to cover the event.

There were coffee and donuts in the anteroom. A diverse lot milled about and introduced each other and shook hands and talked. Pretty secretaries moved briskly through the crowd. I recognized people I'd talked to when I was here two months ago, and one I knew only from his picture. Jubal Hendricks, Senior, had managed Stardrive Labs thirty years ago, when *Snarkhunter #3* was launched. He'd retired just afterward, but here he was, emaciated and tottering, to watch his project's end.

I headed for the coffee table. The man everyone called Butch saw me coming and drew me a cup. He was five feet tall, the color of mahogany, his bright blond hair cut short in a butch cut.

"How good to see you again, Mr. Lane!" He pumped my hand with enthusiasm. "You do remember me?"

"Of course, Butch, very well indeed." I didn't remember his full name, but then, nobody did. And nobody else seemed to want to talk to him. "How have you been?"

"Very well, Mr. Lane, despite my allergies. I have been taking shots."

"They seem to help," I said. Last time I'd seen him his nose had dripped constantly. "Your accent has improved too."

He laughed self-consciously. "It is nearly eight o'clock. Shall we move into the—" His tongue stumbled, and he had to point.

"The auditorium? Yes, let's."

Two months ago we'd been here to catch the first signals from the *Snarkhunter #3* probe as it entered the vicinity of Alpha Centauri. The probe had been flying since before I was born, but that had been its first message since leaving the solar system. On that occasion it had switched itself on on schedule, then given us the sizes and locations of the Centaurus planets.

The speed of light barred us from controlling the *Snarkhunter* from Earth. The probe had been programmed to choose the planet most likely to be earthlike, and to home on it. We had named that planet Centaura, even before we knew it existed . . . thirty years ago, when it was known only that the Centauri suns had planets.

Centaura did exist; we knew that now. For the last two months the *Snarkhunter* should have been moving toward it.

The auditorium hadn't changed much in that time. Stardrive Labs uses the same building for all its publicity on all the probes it currently has flying; but none of those probes had done anything interesting since the *Snarkhuner*'s last report. There were seventy chairs with ashtrays fixed to the backs, set up to face a lighted screen. The screen showed a plot of the *Snarkhunter*'s presumed position with respect to the planet Centaura. Arrows pointed in the directions of Earth and Alpha Centauri A. Naturally the plot was 4.3 years out of date, due to light lag. Hanging from the ceiling were eight TV screens, each presently showing a diagram of the Alpha Centauri A system. In one corner of the big room was a blank sphere eight feet across, with a clear plastic hyperbola mounted near it. *That* was new.

Butch pointed. "The curve is the projected course of the *Snarkhunter*. Mr. Hendricks, Junior, tells me they will draw continents on the sphere as the data arrives."

"Naturally," I said. We found seats. I manfully resisted the urge to smoke, that being one of Butch's allergies.

Time stopped.

I took my coffee in gulps. I'd been up at six o'clock, for the first time in years. My eyes felt gummy; my mouth was centuries old.

Most of the seats were empty. Even under the circumstances, the lack of excitement was remarkable. On screen were a blank circle and a hyperbola and a couple of arrows, and a little rectangle showing the time remaining until perihelion. The rectangle changed every five minutes, and a new point appeared on the hyperbola, showing the new position of the *Snarkhunter* instrument package.

From time to time a blurred radio voice echoed in the auditorium.

"I am amazed," Butch said fervently. "To think that it has come so far! Do you think it will fulfill its purpose?"

"As you say, it's come this far."

"I cannot understand why there is so little excitement."

He couldn't, could he? "It's partly the time lag," I said. "Who can get excited about old news?"

"I suppose so. Still, so much hinges on the success of the project."

"My cup's empty. Can I get you some coffee?"

"Oh, no. No thank you."

I went out and filled my cup, then stayed in the anteroom to smoke a cigarette. Things were happening too slowly. Thirty years the probe had been on its way, but the hours it needed to round Centaura were far too long. Maybe Butch was getting on my nerves.

Not his fault, of course. He was unfailingly polite. You couldn't quarrel with his enthusiasm; it was genuine. It only *seemed* a mockery. And I had to stick with him. Butch's reactions were bigger news by far than the *Snarkhunter* itself.

I spent ten minutes by the coffee dispenser, waiting for interviewees. It was the one sure place to find anyone you wanted to see. I caught Hendricks, Senior, and Hendricks, Junior, Markham who had launched the *Snarkhunter*, and Duryodhana who ran the project now, and several others.

Butch couldn't stand coffee. What had he been doing out here by the coffee dispenser?

Just what I was doing, of course. Waiting for people to speak to him. And nobody wanted to.

I was heading for my seat when the radio cleared its throat.

"We are receiving the carrier wave from *Snarkhunter*. *Snarkhunter* has located Sol and is transmitting correctly. Repeat, location successful. We are now receiving *Snarkhunter*."

The air was full of a two-tone musical note, the sound of the carrier wave, low and sweet.

Butch was hugging his knees in delight. "Wonderful! What is it telling them? Why doesn't he say?"

"The *Snarkhunter* isn't saying anything," I told him. I'd gotten that information from my interviews. "It's just a locator wave to alert us."

"What kind of wave is the probe using?"

"A light beam, a ruby laser. Hear that musical tone? That's the laser, translated into sound and then stepped down to the audible range."

The point on the screen moved another notch. Ten minutes to perihelion.

The radio voice said, "We have received our first burst of data from *Snarkhunter*. Composition of Centaura's atmosphere is as follows. Oxygen sixteen percent, nitrogen eighty-three percent—" It continued detailing carbon dioxide, noble gases, water vapor, ozone, surface pressure, and the planet's surface temperature and magnetic field. Butch hugged his knees and made sounds of pleasure.

"Marvelous!" he enthused. "Marvelous! From such a distance! How sensitive, how versatile the instruments!"

"To me it all seems anticlimactic."

"I fear that is my own fault. I am sorry."

The radio saved me from having to answer. "Decoding of *Snarkhunter*'s transmission is now in progress. In a few minutes we should have a rough map of Centaura's surface." It added, *"Snarkhunter* is about to pass behind the planet. It will reach perihelion three minutes later."

The auditorium became silent. I made a shushing motion at Butch. We heard only the musical sound of the carrier wave.

The sound cut off abruptly.

"It will not reappear," Butch said sadly.

"That's a pity. It was programmed to take another set of measurements at perihelion. They would have been a little more accurate."

The point on the screen moved a notch, to its point of closest approach to Centaura.

"Is that where you shot it down?"

"Yes, at perihelion," said Butch. "How were we to know it was not hostile? We would not have believed it was possible at all. An instrument package, with no external guidance, finding its way over such a distance!" He stood up. "A remarkable achievement! Remarkable! To have done so much with so little!"

"Thanks," I said. Thanks for the pat on the head. "Then you'll go ahead with the trade?"

"I will have to wait," said Butch, "to see if your map of our world is accurate. Thus far your measurements have been excellent. Unbelievably so! If your map is as good, we have a bargain. We will trade you our faster-than-light drive for your incredible probes. Together we will explore space!"

"Fine." I had what I came for. I rose to leave.

"It has been a lonely year," said Butch. "I do not think I knew why until now. Mr. Lane, please don't be offended. Did my landing a year ago cause your people to regard their own technology as inferior?"

"Of course. Why wouldn't it? Our lousy little probe took thirty years to reach Centaura. Your ship took six months! And here you are, like the ghost at the banquet. Oh, damn. I'm sorry, Butch. I lost my head."

"And so you all tend to avoid me. But my own people felt the same way, when your probe reached us four point three years ago. Our faster-than-light drive was a single lucky discovery. Your probe was the combined result of centuries of single-minded, terribly expensive labor and experimentation. We are awed. We are not capable of such sustained effort. But you cannot believe that, can you?"

I couldn't. And I can't.

The
Meddler

SOMEONE was in my room.

It had to be one of Sinc's boys. He'd been stupid. I'd left the lights off. The yellow light now seeping under the door was all the warning I needed.

He hadn't used the door: the threads were still there. That left the fire escape outside the bedroom window.

I pulled my gun, moved back a little in the corridor to get elbow room. Then—I'd practiced it often enough to drive the management crazy—I kicked the door open and was into the room in one smooth motion.

He should have been behind the door, or crouching behind a table, or hidden in the closet with his eye to the keyhole. Instead he was right out in the middle of the living room, facing the wrong way. He'd barely started to turn when I pumped four GyroJet slugs into him. I saw the impacts twitching his shirt. One over the heart.

He was finished.

So I didn't slow down to watch him fall. I crossed the living-room rug in a diving run and landed behind the couch. He couldn't be alone. There had to be others. If one had been behind the couch he might have gotten me, but there wasn't. I scanned the wall behind me, but there was nothing to hide under. So I froze, waiting, listening.

Where were they? The one I'd shot couldn't have come alone.

I was peeved at Sinc. As long as he'd sent goons to waylay me, he might have sent a few who knew what they were doing. The one I'd shot hadn't had time to know he was in a fight.

"Why did you do that?"

Impossibly, the voice came from the middle of the living room, where I'd left a falling corpse. I risked a quick look and brought my head down fast. The afterimage:

He hadn't moved. There was no blood on him. No gun visible, but I hadn't seen his right hand.

Bulletproof vest? Sinc's boys had no rep for that kind of thing, but that had to be it. I stood up suddenly and fired, aiming between the eyes.

The slug smashed his right eye, off by an inch, and I knew he'd shaken me. I dropped back and tried to cool off.

No noises. Still no sign that he wasn't alone.

"I said, 'Why did you do that?' "

Mild curiosity colored his high-pitched voice. He didn't move as I stood up, and there was no hole in either eye.

"Why did I do what?" I asked cleverly.

"Why did you make holes in me? My gratitude for the gift of metal, of course, but—" He stopped suddenly, like he'd said too much and knew it. But I had other worries.

"Anyone else here?"

"Only we two are present. I beg pardon for invasion of privacy, and will indemnify—" He stopped again, as suddenly, and started over. "Who were you expecting?"

"Sinc's boys. I guess they haven't caught on yet. Sinc's boys want to make holes in *me*."

"Why?"

Could he be that stupid? "To turn me off! To kill me!"

He looked surprised, then furious. He was so mad he gurgled. "I should have been informed! Someone has been unforgivably sloppy!"

"Yah. Me. I thought you must be with Sinc. I shouldn't have shot at you. Sorry."

"Nothing," he smiled, instantly calm again.

"But I ruined your suit . . ." I trailed off. Holes showed in his jacket and shirt, but no blood. "Just what *are* you?"

He stood about five feet four, a round little man in an old-fashioned brown one-button suit. There was not a hair on him, not even eyelashes. No warts, no wrinkles, no character lines. A nebbish, one of these guys whose edges are all round, like someone forgot to put in the fine details.

He spread smoothly manicured hands. "I am a man like yourself."

"Nuts."

"Well," he said angrily, "you would have thought so if the preliminary investigation team had done their work properly!"

"You're a—martian?"

"I am *not* a martian. I am—" He gurgled. "Also I am an anthropologist. Your word. I am here to study your species."

"You're from outer space?"

"Very. The direction and distance are secret, of course. My very existence should have been secret." He scowled deeply. Rubber face, I thought, not knowing the half of it yet.

"I won't talk," I reassured him. "But you came at a bad time. Any minute now, Sinc's going to figure out who it is that's on his tail. Then he'll be on mine, and this dump'll be ground zero. I hate to brush you. I've never met a . . . whatever."

"I too must terminate this interview, since you know me for what I am. But first, tell me of your quarrel. Why does Sinc want to make holes in you?"

"His name is Lester Dunhaven Sinclair the third. He runs every racket in this city. Look, we've got time for a drink—maybe. I've got scotch, bourbon—"

He shuddered. "No, I thank you."

"Just trying to set you at ease." I was a little miffed.

"Then perhaps I may adapt a more comfortable form, while you drink—whatever you choose. If you don't mind."

"Please yourself." I went to the rolling bar and poured bourbon and tap water, no ice. The apartment house was dead quiet. I wasn't surprised. I've lived here a couple of years now, and the other tenants have learned the routine. When guns go off, they hide under their beds and stay there.

"You won't be shocked?" My visitor seemed anxious. "If you are shocked, please say so at once."

And he melted. I stood there with the paper cup to my lip and watched him flow out of his one-button suit and take the compact shape of a half-deflated gray beach ball.

I downed the bourbon and poured more, no water. My hands stayed steady.

"I'm a private cop," I told the martian. He'd extruded a convoluted something I decided was an ear. "When Sinc showed up about three years ago and started taking over the rackets, I stayed out of his way. He was the law's business, I figured. Then he bought the law, and that was okay too. I'm no crusader."

"Crusader?" His voice had changed. Now it was deep, and it sounded like something bubbling up from a tar pit.

"Never mind. I tried to stay clear of Sinc, but it didn't work. Sinc had a client of mine killed. Morrison, his name was. I was following Morrison's wife, getting evidence for a divorce. She was shacking up with a guy named Adler. I had all the evidence I needed when Morrison disappeared.

"Then I found out Adler was Sinc's right hand."

"Right hand? Nothing was said of hive cultures."

"Huh?"

"One more thing the prelim team will have to answer for. Continue talking. You fascinate me."

"I kept working on it. What could I do? Morrison was my client, and he was dead. I collected plenty of evidence against Adler, and I turned it over to the cops. Morrison's body never turned up, but I had good corpus delicti evidence. Anyway, Sinc's bodies never do turn up. They just disappear.

"I turned what I had over to the cops. The case was squashed. Somehow the evidence got lost. One night I got beat up."

"Beat up?"

"Almost any kind of impact," I told him, "can damage a human being."

"Really!" he gurgled. "All that water, I suppose."

"Maybe. In my line you have to heal fast. Well, that tore it. I started looking for evidence against Sinc himself. A week ago I sent Xeroxes off to the Feds. I let one of Sinc's boys find a couple of the copies. Bribery evidence, nothing exciting, but enough to hurt. I figured it wouldn't take Sinc long to figure out who made them. The Xerox machine I borrowed was in a building he owns."

"Fascinating. I think I will make holes in the Lady of Preliminary Investigation."

"Will that hurt?"

"She is not a—" Gurgle. "She is a—" Loud, shrill bird whistle.

"I get it. Anyway, you can see how busy I'm going to be. Much too busy to talk about, uh, anthropology. Any minute now I'll have Sinc's boys all over me, and the first one I kill I'll have the cops on me too. Maybe the cops'll come first. I dunno."

"May I watch? I promise not to get in your path."

"Why?"

He cocked his ear, if that was what it was. "An example. Your species has developed an extensive system of engineering using alternating current. We were surprised to find you transmitting electricity so far, and using it in so many ways. Some may even be worth imitating."

"That's nice. So?"

"Perhaps there are other things we can learn from you."

I shook my head. "Sorry, short stuff. This party's bound to get rough, and I don't want any bystanders getting hurt. *What* the hell am I talking about. Holes don't hurt you?"

"Very little hurts me. My ancestors once used genetic engineering to improve their design. My major weaknesses are susceptibility to certain organic poisons, and a voracious appetite."

"Okay, stay then. Maybe after it's all over you can tell me about Mars, or wherever you came from. I'd like that."

"Where I come from is classified. I can tell you about Mars."

"Sure, sure. How'd you like to raid the fridge while we wait? If you're so hungry all the time—hold it."

Sliding footsteps.

They were out there. A handful of them, if they were trying to keep it a secret. And these had to be from Sinc, because all the neighbors were under their beds by now.

The martian heard it too. "What shall I do? I cannot reach human form fast enough."

I was already behind the easy chair. "Then try something else. Something easy."

A moment later I had two matching black leather footstools. They both matched the easy chair, but maybe nobody'd notice.

The door slammed wide open. I didn't pull the trigger, because nobody was there. Just the empty hallway.

The fire escape was outside my bedroom window, but that window was locked and bolted and rigged with alarms. They wouldn't get in that way. Unless—

I whispered, "Hey! How did you get in?"

"Under the door."

So that was all right. The window alarms were still working. "Did any of the tenants see you?"

"No."

"Good." I get enough complaints from the management without *that.*

More faint rustling from outside the door. Then a hand and gun appeared for an instant, fired at random, vanished. Another hole in my walls. He'd had time to see my head, to place me. I ran low for the couch. I was getting set again, both eyes on the door, when a voice behind me said, "Stand up slow."

You had to admire the guy. He'd got through the window alarms without a twitch, into the living room without a sound. He was tall, olive-skinned, with straight black hair and black eyes. His gun was centered on the bridge of my nose.

I dropped the GyroJet and stood up. Pushing it now would only get me killed.

He was very relaxed, very steady. "That's a Gyro-Jet, isn't it? Why not use a regular heater?"

"I like this," I told him. Maybe he'd come too close, or take his eyes off me, or—anything. "It's light as a toy, with no recoil. The gun is just a launching chamber for the rocket slugs, and they pack the punch of a forty-five."

"But, man! The slugs cost a buck forty-five each!"

"I don't shoot that many people."

"At those prices, I believe it. Okay, turn around slow. Hands in the air." His eyes hadn't left me for a moment.

I turned my back. Next would be a sap—

Something metal brushed against my head, feather-light. I whirled, struck at his gun hand and his larynx. Pure habit. I'd moved the instant the touch told me he was in reach.

He was stumbling back with his hand to his throat. I put a fist in his belly and landed the other on his chin. He dropped, trying to curl up. And sure enough, he was holding a sap.

But why hadn't he hit me with it? From the feel of

it, he'd laid it gently on top of my head, carefully, as if he thought the sap might shatter.

"All right, stand easy." The hand and gun came through the doorway, attached to six feet of clean living. I knew him as Handel. He looked like any blond brainless hero, but he wasn't brainless, and he was no hero.

He said, "You're going to hate yourself for doing that."

The footstool behind him began to change shape.

"Dammit," I said, "that's not fair."

Handel looked comically surprised, then smiled winningly. "Two to one?"

"I was talking to my footstool."

"Turn around. We've got orders to bring you to Sinc, if we can. You could still get out of this alive."

I turned around. "I'd like to apologize."

"Save it for Sinc."

"No, honest. It wasn't my idea to have someone else mix in this. Especially—" Again I felt something brush against the side of my head. The martian must be doing something to stop the impact.

I could have taken Handel then. I didn't move. It didn't seem right that I could break Handel's neck when he couldn't touch me. Two to one I don't mind, especially when the other guy's the one. Sometimes I'll even let some civic-minded bystander help, if there's some chance he'll live through it. But *this* . . .

"What's not fair?" asked a high, complaining voice.

Handel screamed like a woman. I turned to see him charge into the door jamb, back up a careful two feet, try for the door again and make it.

Then I saw the footstool.

He was already changing, softening in outline, but I got an idea of the shape Handel had seen. No wonder it had softened his mind. I felt it softening my bones, melting the marrow, and I closed my eyes and whispered, "Dammit, you were supposed to *watch*."

"You told me the impact would damage you."

"That's not the point. Detectives are *always* getting hit on the head. We *expect* it."

"But how can I learn anything from watching you if your little war ends so soon?"

"Well, what do you learn if you keep jumping in?"

"You may open your eyes."

I did. The martian was back to his nebbish form. He had fished a pair of orange shorts out of his pile of clothes. "I do not understand your objection," he said. "This Sinc will kill you if he can. Do you want that?"

"No, but—"

"Do you believe that your side is in the right?"

"Yes, but—"

"Then why should you not accept my help?"

I wasn't sure myself. It felt wrong. It was like sneaking a suitcase bomb into Sinc's mansion and blowing it up.

I thought about it while I checked the hall. Nobody there. I closed the door and braced a chair under the knob. The dark one was still with us: he was trying to sit up.

"Look," I told the martian. "Maybe I can explain, maybe I can't. But if I don't get your word to stay out of this, I'll leave town. I swear it. I'll just drop the whole thing. Understand?"

"No."

"Will you promise?"

"Yes."

The Spanish type was rubbing his throat and staring at the martian. I didn't blame him. Fully dressed, the martian could have passed for a man, but not in a pair of orange undershorts. No hair or nipples marked his 1041 Convergent Series 10-11 x20 tr. ms. 10-23-b flashing white smile on me and asked, "Who's he?"

"I'll ask the questions. Who're you?"

"Don Domingo." His accent was soft and Spanish. If he was worried, it didn't show. "Hey, how come you didn't fall down when I hit you?"

"I said I'll ask the—"

"Your face is turning pink. Are you embarrassed about something?"

"Dammit, Domingo, where's Sinc? Where were you supposed to take me?"

"The place."

"What place? The Bel Air place?"

"That's the one. You know, you have the hardest head—"

"Never mind that!"

"Okay okay. What will you do now?"

I couldn't call the law in. "Tie you up, I guess. After this is over, I'll turn you in for assault."

"After this is over, you won't be doing much, I think. You will live as long as they shoot at your head, but when—"

"Now *drop* that!"

The martian came out of the kitchen. His hand was flowing around a tin of corned beef, engulfing it tin and all. Domingo's eyes went wide and round.

Then the bedroom exploded.

It was a fire bomb. Half the living room was in flames in an instant. I scooped up the GyroJet, stuck it in my pocket.

The second bomb exploded in the hall. A blast of flame blew the door inward, picked up the chair I'd used to brace the door and flung it across the room.

"No!" Domingo yelled. "Handel was supposed to wait! *Now* what?"

Now we roast, I thought, stumbling back with my arm raised against the flames. A calm tenor voice asked, "Are you suffering from excessive heat?"

"Yes! Dammit, yes!"

A huge rubber ball slammed into my back, hurling me at the wall. I braced my arms to take up some of the impact. It was still going to knock me silly. Just before I reached it, the wall disappeared. It was the outside wall. Completely off balance, I dashed through an eight-foot hole and out into the empty night, six floors above concrete.

I clenched my teeth on the scream. The ground came up—the ground came up—where the hell was the ground? I opened my eyes. Everything was happening in slow motion. A second stretched to eternity. I had time to see strollers turning to crane upward, and to spot Handel near a corner of the building, holding a handkerchief to his bleeding nose. Time to look over my shoulder as Domingo stood against a flaming background, poised in slow motion in an eight-foot circle cut through the wall of my apartment.

Flame licked him. He jumped.

Slow motion?

He went past me like a falling safe. I saw him hit; I heard him hit. It's not a good sound. Living on Wall Street during November '80, I heard it night after night during the weeks following the election. I never got used to it.

Despite everything my belly and groin were telling me, I was not falling. I was sinking, like through water. By now half a dozen people were watching me settle. They all had their mouths open. Something poked me in the side, and I slapped at it and found myself clutching a .45 slug. I plucked another off my cheek. Handel was shooting at me.

I fired back, not aiming too well. If the martian hadn't been "helping" me I'd have blown his head off without a thought. As it was—anyway, Handel turned and ran.

I touched ground and walked away. A dozen hot, curious eyes bored into my back, but nobody tried to stop me.

There was no sign of the martian. Nothing else followed me either. I spent half an hour going through the usual contortions to shake a tail, but that was just habit. I wound up in a small, anonymous bar.

My eyebrows were gone, giving me a surprised look. I found myself studying my reflection in the bar mirror, looking for other signs that I'd been in a fight.

My face, never particularly handsome, has been dignified by scar tissue over the years, and my light brown hair never wants to stay in place. I had to move the part a year back to match a bullet crease in my scalp. The scars were all there, but I couldn't find any new cuts or bruises. My clothes weren't mussed. I didn't hurt anywhere. It was all unreal and vaguely dissatisfying.

But my next brush with Sinc would be for real.

I had my GyroJet and a sparse handful of rocket slugs in one pocket. Sinc's mansion was guarded like Fort Knox. And Sinc would be expecting me; he knew I wouldn't run.

We knew a lot about each other, considering we'd never met.

Sinc was a teetotaler. Not a fanatic; there was liquor on the premises of his mansion–fort. But it had to be kept out of Sinc's sight.

A woman usually shared his rooms. Sinc's taste was excellent. He changed his women frequently. They never left angry, and that's unusual. They never left poor, either.

I'd dated a couple of Sinc's exes, letting them talk about Sinc if they cared to. The consensus:

Sinc was an all-right guy, a spender, inventive and enthusiastic where it counted.

And neither particularly wanted to go back.

Sinc paid well and in full. He'd bail a man out of jail if the occasion arose. He never crossed anyone. Stranger yet, nobody ever crossed him. I'd had real trouble learning anything about Sinc. Nobody had wanted to talk.

But he'd crossed Domingo. That had caught us both by surprise.

Put it different. Someone had crossed Domingo. Domingo had been waiting for rescue, not bombs. So had I. It was Sinc's policy to pull his boys out if they got burned.

Either Domingo had been crossed against Sinc's orders, or Sinc was serious about wanting me dead.

I meet all kinds of people. I like it that way. By now I knew enough about Sinc to want to know more, much more. I wanted to meet him. And I was damn glad I'd shaken the martian, because . . .

Just what was it that bugged me about the martian?

It wasn't the strangeness. I meet all kinds. The way he shifted shape could throw a guy, but I don't bug easy.

Manners? He was almost too polite. And helpful.

Much too helpful.

That was part of it. The lines of battle had been drawn . . . and then something had stepped in from outer space. He was deus ex machina, the angel who descends on a string to set everything right, and incidentally to ruin the story. Me tackling Sinc with the martian's help was like a cop planting evidence. It was wrong. But more than that, it seemed to rob the thing of all its point, so that nothing mattered.

I shrugged angrily and had another drink. The bartender was trying to close. I drank up fast and walked out in a clump of tired drunks.

My car had tools I could use, but by now there'd be a bomb under the hood. I caught a cab and gave him an address on Bellagio, a couple of blocks from Sinc's place, if you can number anything in that area in "blocks." It's all hills, and the streets can drive you nuts. Sinc's home ground was a lumpy triangle with twisted sides, and big. It must have cost the Moon to landscape. One afternoon I'd walked past it, casing it. I couldn't see anything except through the gate. The fence was covered by thick climbing ivy. There were alarms in the ivy.

I waited till the taxi was gone, then loaded the GyroJet and started walking. That left one rocket slug still in my pocket.

In that neighborhood there was something to duck behind every time a car came by. Trees, hedges, gates with massive stone pillars. When I saw headlights I ducked, in case Sinc's boys were patrolling. A little walking took me to within sight of the ivy fence. Any closer and I'd be spotted.

So I ducked onto the property of one of Sinc's neighbors.

The place was an oddity: a rectangular pool with a dinky poolhouse at one end, a main house that was all right angles, and, between the two, a winding brook with a small bridge across it and trees hanging over the water. The brook must have been there before the house, and some of the trees too. It was a bit of primal wilderness that jarred strangely with all the right angles around it. I stuck with the brook, naturally.

This was the easy part. A burglary rap was the worst that could happen to me.

I found a fence. Beyond was asphalt, streetlamps, and then the ivy barrier to Sinc's domain.

Wire cutters? In the car. I'd be a sitting duck if I tried to go over. It could have been sticky, but I moved along the fence, found a rusty gate, and persuaded the padlock to open for me. Seconds later I was across the street and huddled against the ivy, just where I'd taken the trouble to hunt out a few of the alarms.

Ten minutes later I went over.

Sitting duck? Yes. I had a clear view of the house, huge and mostly dark. In the moment before I dropped, someone would have had a clear view of me, too, framed by lamplight at the top of the fence.

I dropped between inner and outer fence and took a moment to think. I hadn't expected an inner fence. It was four feet of solid brick topped by six feet of wiring; and the wiring had a look of high voltage.

Now what?

Maybe I could find something to short out the fence. But that would alert the house just as I was going over. Still, it might be the best chance.

Or I could go back over the ivy and try the gate defenses. Maybe I could even bluff my way through. Sinc must be as curious about me by now as I was about him. Everything I knew about Sinc was in the present tense. Of his past I knew only that there were no records of his past. But if Sinc had heard about my floating lightly down from a sixth-floor window, not unlike Mary Poppins . . . it might be worth a try. At least I'd live long enough to see what Sinc looked like.

Or—

"Hello. How does your war proceed?"

I sighed. He drifted down beside me, still man-shaped, dressed in a dark suit. I saw my mistake when he got closer. He'd altered his skin color to make a suit, shirt, and tie. At a distance it would pass. Even close up, he had nothing that needed hiding.

"I thought I'd got rid of you," I complained. "Are you bigger?" At a guess, his size had nearly doubled.

"Yes. I became hungry."

"You weren't kidding about your appetite."

"The war," he reminded me. "Are you planning to invade?"

"I was. I didn't know about this fence."

"Shall I—?"

"No! No, you shall not whatever you were thinking about. Just watch!"

"What am I to watch? You have done nothing for several minutes."

"I'll think of something."

"Of course."

"But whatever I do, I won't use your help, now or ever. If you want to watch, fine, be my guest. But don't help."

"I do not understand why not."

"It's like bugging a guy's telephone. Sinc has certain rights, even if he is a crook. He's immune from cruel and unusual punishment. The FBI can't bug his phone. You can't kill him unless you try him first, unless he's breaking a law at the time. And he shouldn't have to worry about armed attack by martians!"

"Surely if Sinc himself breaks the rules—"

"There are *rules* for dealing with lawbreakers!" I snapped.

The martian didn't answer. He stood beside me,

seven feet tall and pudgy, a dark, manlike shape in the dim light from the house.

"Hey. How do you do all those things you do? Just a talent?"

"No. I carry implements." Something poked itself out of his baby-smooth chest, something hard that gleamed like metal. "This, for instance, damps momentum. Other portable artifacts lessen the pull of gravity, or reprocess the air in my lung."

"You keep them all inside you?"

"Why not? I can make fingers of all sizes inside me."

"Oh."

"You have said that there are rules for dealing with rule breakers. Surely you have already broken those rules. You have trespassed on private property. You have departed the scene of an accident, Don Domingo's death. You have—"

"All right."

"Then—"

"All right, I'll try again." I was wasting too much time. Getting over the fence was important. But so, somehow, was this. Because in a sense the martian was right. This had nothing to do with rules . . .

"It has nothing to do with rules," I told him. "At least, not exactly. What counts is power. Sinc has taken over this city, and he'll want others too, later. He's got too much power. That's why someone has to stop him.

"And you give me too much power. A—a man who has too much power loses his head. I don't trust myself with you on my side. I'm a detective. If I break a law I expect to be jailed for it unless I can explain why. It makes me careful. If I tackle a crook who can whip me, I get bruised. If I shoot someone who doesn't deserve it, I go to prison. It all tends to make me careful. But with you around—"

"You lose your caution," said the dark bulk beside me. He spoke almost musingly, with more of human expression than I'd heard before. "You may be tempted to take more power than is good for you. I had not expected your species to be so wise."

"You thought we were stupid?"

"Perhaps. I had expected you to be grateful and eager for any help I might give. Now I begin to understand your attitude. We, too, try to balance out the amount of power given to individuals. What is that noise?"

It was a rustling, a scampering, barely audible but not at all furtive.

"I don't know."

"Have you decided upon your next move?"

"Yes. I—damn! Those are dogs!"

"What are dogs?"

Suddenly they were there. In the dark I couldn't tell what breed, but they were big, and they didn't bark. In a rustling of claws scrabbling on cement, they rounded the curve of the brick wall, coming from both sides, terribly fast. I hefted the GyroJet and knew there were twice as many dogs as I had shots.

Lights came on, bright and sudden, all over the grounds. I fired, and a finger of flame reached out and touched one of the dogs. He fell, tumbling, lost in the pack.

All the lights went deep red, blood red. The dogs stopped. The noise stopped. One dog, the nearest, was completely off the ground, hovering in mid-leap, his lips skinned back from sharp ruby teeth.

"It seems I have cost you time," the martian murmured. "May I return it?"

"What did you do?"

"I have used the damper of inertia in a projected field. The effect is as if time has stopped for all but us. In view of the length of time I have kept you talking, it is the least I can do."

Dogs to the left and dogs to the right, and lights all the hell over the place. I found men with rifles placed like statues about the wide lawn.

"I don't know if you're right or wrong," I said. "I'll

be dead if you turn off that time stopper. But this is the last time. Okay?"

"Okay. We will use only the inertia damper."

"I'll move around to the other side of the house. Then you turn off the gadget. It'll give me some time to find a tree."

We went. I stepped carefully among the statues of dogs. The martian floated behind like a gigantic, pudgy ghost.

The channel between inner and outer fence went all the way around to the gate at the front of the house. Near the gate the inner fence pinched against the outer, and ended. But before we reached that point I found a tree. It was big and it was old, and one thick branch stretched above the fence to hover over our heads.

"Okay, turn off the gadget."

The deep red lights glared a sudden white.

I went up the ivy. Long arms and oversized hands are a big help to my famous monkey act. No point now in worrying about alarms. I had to balance standing on the outer fence to reach the branch with my fingers. When I put my weight on it it dipped three feet and started to creak. I moved along hand over hand, and swung up into the leaves before my feet could brush the inner fence. At a comfortable crotch I settled myself to take stock.

There were at least three riflemen on the front lawn. They were moving in a search pattern, but they didn't expect to find anything. All the action was supposed to be in back.

The martian floated into the air and moved across the fence.

He nicked the top going over. A blue spark snapped, and he dropped like a sack of wheat. He landed against the fence, grounded now, and electricity leaped and sizzled. Ozone and burnt meat mixed in the cold night air. I dropped out of the tree and ran to him. I didn't touch him. The current would have killed me.

It had certainly killed him.

And that was something I'd never thought of. Bullets didn't faze him. He could produce miracles on demand. How could he be killed by a simple electric fence? If he'd only mentioned that! But he'd been surprised even to find that we had electricity.

I'd let a bystander be killed. The one thing I'd sworn I would never do again . . .

Now he was nothing like human. Metal things poked gleaming from the dead mass that had been an anthropologist from the stars. The rustle of current had stopped seconds ago. I pulled one of the metal gadgets out of the mass, slid it in a pocket, and ran.

They spotted me right away. I took a zigzag course around a fenced tennis court, running for the front door. There were man-length windows on either side of the door. I ran up the steps, brought the GyroJet down in a hurried slashing blow that broke most of the panes in one window, and dove off the steps into a line of bushes.

When things happen that fast, your mind has to fill the gaps between what you saw and what you didn't. All three gunmen chased me frantically up the steps and through the front door, shouting at the tops of their lungs.

I moved along the side of the house, looking for a window.

Somebody must have decided I couldn't go through all that jagged glass. He must have outshouted the others, too, because I heard the hunt start again. I climbed a piece of wall, found a little ledge outside a darkened second-floor window. I got the window up without too much noise.

For the first time on this crazy night, I was beginning to think I knew what I was doing. That seemed odd, because I didn't know much about the layout of the house, and I hadn't the faintest idea where I was. But at least I knew the rules of the game. The variable, the martian, the deus ex machina, was out of the picture.

The rules were: whoever saw me would kill me if he could. No bystanders, no good guys would be here tonight. There would be no complex moral choices. I would not be offered supernatural help, in return for my soul or otherwise. All I had to do was try to stay alive.

(But a bystander had died.)

The bedroom was empty. Two doors led to a closet and a bathroom. Yellow light seeped under a third door. No choice here. I pulled the GyroJet and eased the third door open.

A face jerked up over the edge of a reading chair. I showed it the gun, kept it aimed as I walked around in front of the chair. Nobody else was in the room.

The face could have used a shave. It was beefy, middle-aged, but symmetrical enough except for an oversized nose. "I know you," it said, calmly enough considering the circumstances.

"I know you too." It was Adler, the one who'd gotten me into this mess, first by cohabiting with Morrison's wife and then by killing Morrison.

"You're the guy Morrison hired," said Adler. "The tough private eye. Bruce Cheseborough. Why couldn't you let well enough alone?"

"I couldn't afford to."

"You couldn't afford not to. Have some coffee."

"Thanks. You know what'll happen if you yell or anything?"

"Sure." He picked up a water glass, dumped the water in the wastebasket. He picked up a silver thermos and poured coffee into his own coffee cup and into the water glass, moving slowly and evenly. He didn't want to make me nervous.

He himself was no more than mildly worried. That was reassuring, in a way, because he probably wouldn't do anything stupid. But . . . I'd seen this same calm in Don Domingo, and I knew the cause. Adler and Domingo and everyone else who worked for Sinc, they all had perfect faith in him. Whatever trouble they were in, Sinc would get them out.

I watched Adler take a healthy gulp of coffee before I touched the glass. The coffee was black and strong, heavily laced with good brandy. My first gulp tasted so good I damn near smiled at Adler.

Adler smiled back. His eyes were wide and fixed, as if he were afraid to look away from me. As if he expected me to explode. I tried to think of a way he could have dropped something in the coffee without drinking it himself. There wasn't any.

"You made a mistake," I told him, and gulped more coffee. "If my name had been Rip Hammer or Mike Hero, I might have dropped the whole thing when I found out you were with Sinc's boys. But when your name is Bruce Cheseborough, Junior, you can't afford to back out of a fight."

"You should have. You might have lived." He said it without concentrating on it. A puzzled frown tugged at the corners of his eyes and mouth. He was still waiting for something to happen.

"Tell you what. You write me out a confession, and I can leave here without killing anyone. Won't that be nice?"

"Sure. What should I confess to?"

"Killing Morrison."

"You don't expect me to do that."

"Not really."

"I'm going to surprise you." Adler got up, still slow, and went behind the desk. He kept his hands high until I was around behind him. "I'll write your damn confession. You know why? Because you'll never use it. Sinc'll see to that."

"If anyone comes through that door—"

"I know, I know." He started writing. While he was at it, I examined the tool I'd taken from the martian's corpse. It was white shiny metal, with a complex shape that was like nothing I'd ever seen. Like the plastic guts in a toy gun, half melted and then cooled, so that all the parts were merged and rounded. I had no idea what it did. Anyway, it was no good to me. I could see slots where buttons or triggers were buried, but they were too small for fingers. Tweezers might have reached them, or a hatpin.

Adler handed me the paper he'd been writing on. He'd made it short and pointed: motive, means, details of time. Most of it I already knew.

"You don't say what happened to the body."

"Same thing that happened to Domingo."

"Domingo?"

"Domingo, sure. When the cops came to pick him up in back of your place, he was gone. Even the bloodstains were gone. A miracle, right?" Adler smiled nastily. When I didn't react he looked puzzled.

"How?" I asked him.

Adler shrugged uncomfortably. "You already know, don't you? I won't write it down. It would bring Sinc in. You'll have to settle for what you've got."

"Okay. Now I tie you up and wend my way homeward."

Adler was startled. He couldn't have faked it. "Now?"

"Sure. You killed my client, not Sinc."

He grinned, not believing me. And he still thought something was about to happen.

I used the bathrobe sash for his arms and a handkerchief for a gag. There were other bathrobes in the closet to finish the job. He still didn't believe I was going to leave, and he was still waiting for something to happen. I left him on the bed, in the dark.

Now what?

I turned off the lights in the sitting room and went to the window. The lawn was alive with men and dogs and far too much light. That was the direct way out.

I had Adler's hide in my pocket. Adler, who had killed my client. Was I still chasing Sinc? Or should I try to get clear with that piece of paper?

Get clear, of course.

I stood by the window, picking out shadows. There was a lot of light, but the shadows of bushes and trees were jet black. I found a line of hedge, lighted on this side; but I could try the other. Or move along *that* side of the tennis court, then hop across to *that* odd-looking statue—

The door opened suddenly, and I whirled.

A man in dark slacks and a smoking jacket stood facing my gun. Unhurriedly, he stepped through the door and closed it behind him.

It was Sinc. Lester Dunhaven Sinclair III was a man in perfect condition, not a pound overweight or underweight, with gymnasium muscles. I guessed his age at thirty-four or so. Once before I'd seen him, in public, but never close enough to see what I saw now: that his thick blond hair was a wig.

He smiled at me. "Cheseborough, isn't it?"

"Yah."

"What did you do with my . . . lieutenant?" He looked me up and down. "I gather he's still with us."

"In the bedroom. Tied up." I moved around to lock the door to the hall.

I understood now why Sinc's men had made him into something like a feudal overlord. He measured up. He inspired confidence. His confidence in himself was total. Looking at him, I could almost believe that nothing could stand against him.

"I gather you were too intelligent to try the coffee. A pity," said Sinc. He seemed to be examining my gun, but with no trace of fear. I tried to think it was a bluff, but I couldn't. No man could put across such a bluff. His twitching muscles would give him away. I began to be afraid of Sinc.

"A pity," he repeated. "Every night for the past year Adler has gone to bed with a pot of coffee spiked with brandy. Handel too."

What was he talking about? The coffee hadn't affected me at all. "You've lost me," I said.

"Have I?" Smiling as if he'd won a victory, Sinc began to gurgle. It was eerily familiar, that gurgle. I felt the rules changing again, too fast to follow. Smiling, gurgling rhythmically, Sinc put a hand in his pants pocket and pulled out an automatic. He took his time about it.

It was not a big gun, but it was a gun; and the moment I knew that, I fired.

A GyroJet rocket slug burns its solid fuel in the first twenty-five feet, and moves from there on momentum. Sinc was twenty-five feet away. Flame reached out to tap him on the shoulder joint, and Sinc smiled indulgently. His gun was steady on the bridge of my nose.

I fired at his heart. No effect. The third shot perforated the space between his eyes. I saw the hole close, and I knew. Sinc was cheating too.

He fired.

I blinked. Cold fluid trickled down from my forehead, stung my eyes, dribbled across my lips. I tasted rubbing alcohol.

"You're a martian too," I said.

"No need for insult," Sinc said mildly. He fired again. The gun was a squirtgun, a plastic kid's toy shaped like an automatic. I wiped the alcohol out of my eyes and looked at him.

"Well," said Sinc. "Well." He reached up, peeled his hair off, and dropped it. He did the same with his eyebrows and eyelashes. "Well, where is he?"

"He told me he was an . . . anthropologist. Was he lying?"

"Sure, Cheseborough. He was the Man. The Law. He's tracked me over distances you couldn't even write down." Sinc backed up against a wall. "You wouldn't even understand what my people called my crime. And you've no reason to protect him. He used you. Every time he stopped a bullet for you, it was to make me think you were him. That's why he helped you on a floating act. That's why he's disposed of Domingo's body. You were his stalking-horse. I'm supposed to kill you while he's sneaking up on me. He'll sacrifice you without a qualm. Now *where is he?*"

"Dead. He didn't know about electric fences."

A voice from the hall, Handel's voice, bellowed, "Mr. Sinclair! Are you all right in there?"

"I have a guest," Sinc called out. "He has a gun."

"What do we do?"

"Don't do anything," Sinc called to him. And then he started to laugh. He was losing his human contours, "relaxing" because I already knew what he was.

"I wouldn't have believed it," he chuckled. "He tracked me all that way to die on an electric fence!" His chuckles cut off like a broken tape, making me wonder how real they were, how real his laughter could be with his no doubt wierd breathing system. "The current couldn't kill him, of course. It must have shorted his airmaker and blown the battery."

"The spiked coffee was for him," I guessed. "He said he could be killed by organic poisons. He meant alcohol."

"Obviously. And all I did was give you a free drink," he chuckled.

"I've been pretty gullible. I believed what your women told me."

"*They* didn't know." He did a pretty accurate double take. "You thought . . . Cheseborough, have I made rude comments about your sex life?"

"No. Why?"

"Then you can leave mine alone."

He had to be kidding. No he didn't; he could take any shape he liked. Wow, I thought. Sinc's really gone native. Maybe he *was* laughing, or thought he was.

Sinc moved slowly toward me. I backed away, holding the useless gun.

"You realize what happens now?"

I took a guess. "Same thing that happened to Domingo's body. All your embarrassing bodies."

"Exactly. Our species is known for its enormous appetite." He moved toward me, the squirt gun forgotten in his right hand. His muscles had sagged and smoothed. Now he was like the first step in making a clay model of a man. But his mouth was growing larger, and his teeth were two sharp-edged horseshoes.

I fired once more.

Something smashed heavily against the door. Sinc didn't hear it. Sinc was melting, losing all form as he tried to wrap himself around his agony. From the fragments of his shattered plastic squirt gun, rubbing alcohol poured over what had been his hand and dripped to the floor.

The door boomed again. Something splintered.

Sinc's hand was bubbling, boiling. Sinc, screaming, was flowing out of his slacks and smoking jacket. And I . . . I snapped out of whatever force was holding me rooted, and I picked up the silver thermos and poured hot spiked coffee over whatever it was that writhed on the floor.

Sinc bubbled all over. White metal machinery extruded itself from the mass and lay on the rug.

The door crackled and gave. By then I was against the wall, ready to shoot anything that looked my way. Handel burst into the room and stopped dead.

He stood there in the doorway, while the stars grew old and went out. Nothing, I felt, could have torn his eyes from that twitching, bubbling mass. Gradually the mass stopped moving . . . and Handel gulped, got his throat working, shrieked, and ran from the room.

I heard the meaty thud as he collided with a guard, and I heard him babbling, "Don't go in there! Don't . . . oh, don't . . ." and then a sob, and the sound of uneven running feet.

I went into the bedroom and out the window. The grounds still blazed with light, but I saw no motion. Anyway, there was nothing out there but dogs and men.

Dry
Run

BY habit Simpson was a one-hand driver. On this day he drove with both hands wrapped tight around the wheel, strangling it. He looked straight ahead, down the curving length of the freeway, and he stayed in the right-center lane.

He wanted a cigarette; yet he was almost afraid to let go of the wheel. The air-conditioning nozzle blew icy air up at his face and down at his belt buckle; icy because of the way he was perspiring. He felt the weakness in his bowels, and he cursed silently, trying to relax.

The dog in the trunk—

Too late now, too late to change his mind—

He stabbed a finger at the cigarette lighter, missed —Jesus! He'd only been driving the Buick for five years!—found it and pushed it in. He fumbled a Camel from the central glove compartment, one-handed, without looking. Traffic was not too heavy. It was past seven o'clock, though the July sun was still a falling glory below red streamers of cloud. A few cars had their lights on, unnecessarily. Were the drivers afraid they'd forget later? The cars in this lane were doing sixty to sixty-five. Usually Simpson chose the fast lane. This time was different. No risks on this trip.

Too late now, too late to back out. He wouldn't if he could. He lit the cigarette, dragged, put the lighter back, and gripped the wheel again with both hands. The cigarette bent and flattened between his fingers.

Red taillights. This lane was slowing. He touched the brake with his foot, eased down, harder. Hard! He tried to push the brake through the floor. He stopped a foot behind a vintage Cadillac, and stalled. Simpson swore and turned the ignition hard over. The motor caught instantly.

It didn't matter. Nobody was moving.

Overhead were the swooping concrete noodles of the Santa Monica Freeway ramps. A carpet of cars was stalled underneath, stalled for as far ahead as Simpson could see. Then there was motion in the distance. He waited.

The vintage Cadillac jerked half a car length forward. Simpson followed. Another ripple of motion, another car length forward.

The freeway shouldn't be this crowded. Seven-thirty on a week night? He'd picked his time carefully enough. What was happening?

The Cad moved again. Its driver looked back over his shoulder: angry, middle-aged, sweaty, and somewhat overweight. He looked like he'd bite anyone who came close enough.

Simpson felt the same way. He eased forward . . .

Murray Simpson was six inches too tall for the driver's seat of the Buick. He banged his elbows and knees getting in and out. The driver's seat cramped his legs, bending them too far at the knee, even when it was as far back as it would go.

In repose he always looked unhappy. He had that kind of face. His most genuine laughter looked forced. See him now, stalled in a traffic jam on the San Diego Freeway in a car too small for him. Stalled partway through a murder plan which was too complex to begin with . . .

He looked frantic. His brown eyes burned; his

no-color hair had lost all semblance of civilization. His forgotten cigarette burned threateningly between white knuckles.

Ahead of the blue Cadillac was a Jaguar convertible whose custom paint job glowed with fiery tangerine brilliance. Ahead of that, a long gray anonymous Detroit car with huge delta fins. The gray car was stalled.

Someone behind Simpson was honking madly.

Cars poured into the gap in his lane, the gap ahead of the stalled car.

At Hermosa Beach the red tide was in. Trillions and quadrillions of plankton made a dirty red-and-brown soup of the ocean. By night the breakers glowed with cold blue fire. By night and day, the ocean air stank of too much life.

In the trunk of the Buick, Simpson's dun-colored Great Dane lay dead with a hole in his head. He was beginning to stiffen.

No room to get out of this lane. Simpson clenched his teeth and clung to his temper. Part of him wanted to stamp on the throttle and swoop out into the next lane, and damn the car that got in his way! But there was Harvey in the trunk, with his head in a Baggy. Simpson lit another cigarette.

What was Janet doing now? Who was she with? Did Simpson know him? No; Janet wasn't stupid, nor was the divorce yet final. Anyone with her now would be female.

Had she missed Harvey yet? Was she searching for him now, wondering how he'd got out, hoping he hadn't reached the street?

How would Janet look in the trunk of the Buick, with her head in a Baggy to hold the blood?

Cars swept by on the left and right, going ten and fifteen miles per hour.

A woman in a peach-colored dress got out of the gray car and opened the hood. She fiddled in the guts of the motor, then got back in. The gray car lurched forward.

She'd fixed it! Amazing!

And the whole lane crawled off at ten miles per hour, southbound on the San Diego Freeway. Toward Simpson's tiny house on the Strand at Hermosa Beach.

Driving was torture. Ripples crawled backward along the lines of cars. Some deadhead in front was moving in spurts, and the spurts became waves traveling backward, communicating their motion to every car behind him. Accelerator, brake, accelerator, brake. Brake! Accelerate. Maddeningly slow. There was the car that had blocked the lanes, twisted across the right lanes with its side smashed in, a police car alongside. Now the lanes moved faster.

On Simpson's left they were getting up to speed. Simpson saw a gap. He twisted the wheel, depressed the throttle, and looked quickly over his shoulder. Nobody coming . . . he stamped on the throttle and brought his eyes back to the road.

Every car in his lane must have stopped dead the moment he turned his head. His foot was still on the throttle when he hit.

Discontinuity. He knew he was about to crash . . . and he was getting out to look at the damage. He'd bumped his head, and his ribs must have smacked hard into the steering wheel, but he had no trouble walking.

He walked through a nightmare.

The Buick's hood looked like a squashed banana. The fat man in the Cadillac was getting out, rubbing his thick neck, his eyes squinted against pain. Whiplash, thought Simpson, and moved toward him.

Then the weakness came, and Simpson dropped hard on his knees. The shock should have hurt, but it didn't. "Sorry," Simpson told the man. *Sorry about your car, your neck. Sorry to be such a fool. Sorry, I feel weak. Sorry.* He fainted.

He knew he had fainted, though he had not felt

his chin hit concrete. Now, without transition, he was totally alert. But alert to what?

There was darkness around him, and a lack of sensation. No sound. Nothing to see or feel. No up or down. The position of his body was a mystery. He visualized himself in a hospital bed, his spinal cord severed at the neck, his eyes bandaged. The thought should have frightened him. It didn't.

Once he'd smoked marijuana. It was unplanned; he'd seen some friends smoking a small-bowled cigarette pipe, using a mechanical roller to make their own cigarettes, and curiosity had got the better of him. He remembered the awful taste at the back of his nose, and the deep, all-embracing peace, and a queer somatic hallucination: the feeling that all the mass of his body had withdrawn into his feet, below a line drawn at the ankles. It seemed that he could lean as far as he liked in any direction and he would not fall, because his center of mass was only an inch above the floor.

The deep peace was the same, but now his body was entirely massless. As before, his memory was unimpaired. The body in the trunk, the crash . . . how, now, could he keep Harvey's death a secret? . . . But it didn't seem to matter.

Suddenly he knew why.

He was dead. Murray Simpson was a dead issue, an embarrassing mass of tissue associated with an equally embarrassing mass of torn metal. And that didn't matter either.

The voice spoke close in front of him. "That was silly, Simpson."

Simpson tried to move. Massless body? He had no body at all. He was a viewpoint. Blind, motionless, without sensation . . . he waited.

"The worst possible time to die is when you're involved in a murder." There was no character to that voice, no accent, no timbre, no emphasis, no loudness or softness. It was neither sharp nor dull, neither hoarse nor smooth. A voice with no *handle*. Like print in a typewriter, that voice.

Simpson said, "Murder?" To his own horror, his voice was exactly like the other's.

"Do you deny it?"

"I admit to killing a dog. My own dog, Harvey, a Great Dane."

"Not your own. Harvey belonged to you and to Janet Grey Simpson, your wife. Your wife has had possession of Harvey for seven months, ever since the two of you separated. Do you deny your intent to commit murder?"

Life after death. Reward and punishment? Simpson said, "I refuse to answer. Are you my judge?"

"No. Another will judge you. I collect only evidence, and you."

Simpson didn't answer. The strange peace was still with him, and he felt that he'd already found the right answer.

"Well, we must find out," said the voiceless voice.

What a weird nightmare, Simpson thought, and tried to pull himself awake. *I dreamed I was in an accident . . . at the worst possible time . . . I'd already killed Harvey . . . poor Harvey. Why would I pick Harvey?* There were voices around him.

Cold reality touched him, icy cold, icy and rough against his cheek. He lay on hard concrete. His chin hurt, and his belly hurt below the edge of his rib cage.

He looked up into the face of a policeman. "Am I dying?"

"Ambulance will be here . . . moment."

The car! Harvey! He tried to say, "What did you do with the car?"

The policeman spoke calmly. " . . . Take it to . . . get it whenever . . . address . . ." His voice faded in and out. And out.

He woke again, thinking, *nightmare!* And again it

was too real. There was a cloth under his cheek. Someone had been a good Samaritan.

He asked nobody, "Am I dying?"

"Just take it easy." Two men folded his arms around him and picked him up in a peculiar grip that supported his innards. The pain under his ribs was not great, but it felt unnatural, terrifying.

"I think he could walk himself," said one.

"I don't dare," Simpson got out, trying to convey his fear. *Something broken in my belly or in my skull. Broken, bleeding, slowly bleeding away my life with nothing to show on the outside.* He was convinced he was dying. It was all that remained of a part of the nightmare that he could not visualize at all.

The men put him on a stretcher and unfolded him into prone position.

The rest of it was hazy. The ride in the ambulance, the doctor asking him questions, the same questions asked earlier by the police. Questions he answered without thought, almost without memory. He didn't become fully aware until an intern said, "Nothing broken. Just bruises."

Simpson was startled. "Are you sure?"

"Have your own doctor take a look tomorrow. For tonight you'll be all right. No broken bones. Is that the only pain, under your ribs?"

"My chin hurts."

"Oh, that's just a scrape. Did you faint?"

"Yes."

"Probably got it then. You're lucky, you know. Your spleen is right under those bruised ribs."

"Jesus."

"You think you can get up? Your wife is coming for you."

Janet, coming here? Janet! "I'll take a taxi," said Simpson. He rolled onto his side, sat up on the high operating table and climbed down to the floor, treating himself like a sackful of expensive raw eggs. "Where did they take my car?"

"The police gave me the address." The man tapped his pockets. One crackled. "Here."

Simpson took the slip, looked at it and shoved it in his pocket. There was a chance he could get the car transferred to his own company before the police looked in the trunk. Or was there? They might have looked already.

What would the police do about a Great Dane with a bullet in his head?

Undoubtedly they'd tell Janet.

He must get the car tomorrow.

The intern showed him to a telephone and loaned him a cigarette. After he called the cab, someone else showed him where to wait. He'd waited five minutes when Janet came.

Her hair was back to auburn. The dress she wore was severe, almost a suit, and it was new. She looked competent and sure of herself.

"How did you know?" he asked her.

"How do you think? The police called my house. They must have found the number on your license, if you didn't tell them."

"I've got a taxi coming."

"Let it come. You're going with me. How did you manage to bang yourself up?"

"There was a traffic jam. I got—"

"Can you stand up?"

She was always interrupting. Once he'd thought she did it deliberately. Once she had, perhaps, but it was a habit she'd never lose.

He stood. The pain under his ribs made him walk carefully. He dreaded what it would feel like tomorrow.

"I'll take you to the beach," she said.

"Okay."

He lived in the beach house now. Janet had been awarded the main house.

He reached the car by leaning on Janet's shoulder. The touch of her was disturbing, and her perfume

roused sharp memories. Aside from premarital prosti-
tutes, he had never carnally known a woman other
than Janet. Now she distracted him, and he kept landing hard on his feet and jarring his ribs. But her
strength was an asset in settling him into the passenger seat.

"Now. How did it happen?"

He told her, in detail. Reaction made him want to
babble. Somehow he managed to leave the dog out of
it. But he told her how sure he had been that he was
going to die, and he spoke of his surprise when the intern told him he wasn't. By the time he finished they
were back on the freeway.

The lights, the flying lights . . . He planted his feet
and tried to push himself through the seat. Janet
didn't notice.

"Harvey's missing," she said.

He should have said, "Oh?"

Instead, he stopped with the word on his lips. He
had suddenly realized that it didn't matter. It hadn't
mattered since the accident, though he hadn't realized it until now.

"I killed Harvey," he said.

She glanced across at him, with distaste. She didn't
believe him.

"He's in the trunk of my car. That's why I was in
such a hurry tonight."

"That's ridiculous. You *like* Harvey."

"It was a sort of dry run. I was planning to kill you."

"I don't understand."

"I had it all planned out," he said. "There's a red
tide down at the beach. Maybe you knew."

"No." She was beginning to believe him, he
thought.

"At night it's lovely. The breakers glow like blue
fire. In the daytime it stinks, and the water's filthy. I
could bury a body anywhere on the beach, and nobody would notice the smell. But I had to know I
could go through with it. Wouldn't I be seven kinds
of idiot if I murdered you and then froze up?"

"Yes," she said, very coldly.

"So I went up to the house and shot Harvey. It was sort of a dry run. If it had worked, you would have been next. The gun in the pillow, the drive to the beach—"

"What an idiotic idea. Didn't it occur to you that they'd search harder for a missing woman than a missing dog?"

"Well—"

"And why Harvey? Why not pick up a dog at the pound? Suppose they were searching for my body on the beach and found Harvey's instead. They'd trace me right to you! Then they'd know they were on the right track!"

"I—"

"I suppose you planned to use the same gun on us both?"

"Yes, I did, as a—"

"And how long do you think a red tide lasts, anyway?"

"The ocean always stinks. There's always a breeze, too."

"Remember the seal that washed up last year? It probably weighed less than seventy pounds. Remember the smell? Think how much worse—"

"All right, all right! It was a stupid plan!"

The angry silence was very, very familiar. It didn't help Simpson to know that his wife was probably right. It never had.

They turned toward the beach. Janet asked, "Why would you want to kill me?"

"The alimony's bleeding me white."

"That's all?"

"No. Personal reasons."

She laughed. He had wondered before: was her laughter always scornful, or did it only sound that way? "My God, Murray! Surely you can tell me, your intended victim!" She sobered suddenly. "Never mind. I don't want to know why. Do you still plan to kill me?"

"No. Not after that."

"The accident."

"Of course. I don't have the nerve. Suppose I . . . did it, and then froze up? My car's in a police lot with a dog's body in the trunk. Well, that won't get me killed. But suppose it was you?"

"That's almost funny," said Janet.

"Want a real laugh? I may never drive the freeway again, either. I was so *sure* I was dying . . ."

"I think I'd better tell someone else about this conversation, just in case."

"Go ahead then," said Simpson. And he had an odd thought: this was his last chance to go through with it. Before she told someone.

And then, an odder thought. Her tone: too light. She still didn't believe him. He was beginning to doubt it himself. Had he really intended to kill Janet?

She'd hurt him badly. She'd hurt him by leaving him: she, the only woman for Murray Simpson. She might as well have taken his testicles along. And he wanted to hurt her, badly.

They had reached the house. Janet pulled into the garage and shut off the ignition. "Do you always leave the door open?"

"Sometimes I forget."

Very uncomfortably, Janet asked, "Shall I come in and make you some coffee?"

"No. No thanks." Simpson opened the door and got out.

And felt it end.

Deep peace. Massless body, without sensation. The darkness of the blind.

Simpson said, "What happened?"

"You didn't kill her," said the voice without character.

"No, of course not. Am I dead again?"

"You are dead, still."

"How?"

"Loss of blood through a ruptured spleen, symptoms masked by shock. Your most recent memories were a dry run. Simpson, you did not kill your wife."

With abstracted logic, Simpson said, "But I would have, if there hadn't been an accident."

"That is debatable. In any case, it was your own accident. You caused it without help."

"Deliberately?" Simpson didn't know.

"Your judge will decide. Shall we go?"

"Yes."

They went.

Convergent
Series

I graduated college with a B.A. in mathematics and a minor in psychology. This peculiar combination is easy to explain. I spent two years taking courses for fun. Then I looked for the quickest way to graduate, and that's what came out.

The mathematics background has been useful, of course. But "Convergent Series" is my only story to have derived directly from mathematics.

IT was a girl in my anthropology class who got me interested in magic. Her name was Ann, and she called herself a white witch, though I never saw her work an effective spell. She lost interest in me and married somebody, at which point I lost interest in her; but by that time magic had become the subject of my thesis in anthropology. I couldn't quit, and wouldn't if I could. Magic fascinated me.

The thesis was due in a month. I had a hundred pages of notes on primitive, medieval, oriental, and modern magic. Modern magic meaning psionics devices and such. Did you know that certain African tribes don't believe in natural death? To them, *every* death is due to witchcraft, and in every case the witch must be found and killed. Some of these tribes are actually dying out due to the number of witchcraft trials and executions. Medieval Europe was just as bad in many ways, but they stopped in time . . . I'd tried several ways of conjuring Christian and other demons, purely in a spirit of research, and I'd put a Taoist curse on Professor Pauling. It hadn't worked. Mrs. Miller was letting me use the apartment-house basement for experiments.

Notes I had, but somehow the thesis wouldn't move. I knew why. For all I'd learned, I had nothing original to say about anything. It wouldn't have stopped everyone (remember the guy who counted every *I* in *Robinson Crusoe?*) but it stopped me. Until one Thursday night—

I get the damndest ideas in bars. This one was a beaut. The bartender got my untouched drink as a tip. I went straight home and typed for four solid hours. It was ten minutes to twelve when I quit, but I now had a complete outline for my thesis, based on a genuinely new idea in Christian witchcraft. All I'd needed was a hook to hang my knowledge on. I stood up and stretched . . .

. . . And knew I'd have to try it out.

All my equipment was in Mrs. Miller's basement, most of it already set up. I'd left a pentagram on the floor two nights ago. I erased that with a wet rag, a former washcloth, wrapped around a wooden block. Robes, special candles, lists of spells, new pentagram . . . I worked quietly so as not to wake anyone. Mrs. Miller was sympathetic; her sense of humor was such that they'd have burned her three centuries ago. But the other residents needed their sleep. I started the incantations exactly at midnight.

At fourteen past I got the shock of my young life. Suddenly there was a demon spread-eagled in the pentagram, with his hands and feet and head occupying all five points of the figure.

I turned and ran.

He roared, "Come back here!"

I stopped halfway up the stairs, turned, and came

back down. To leave a demon trapped in the basement of Mrs. Miller's apartment house was out of the question. With that amplified basso profundo voice he'd have wakened the whole block.

He watched me come slowly down the stairs. Except for the horns he might have been a nude middle-aged man, shaved and painted bright red. But if he'd been human you wouldn't have wanted to know him. He seemed built for all of the Seven Deadly Sins. Avaricious green eyes. Enormous gluttonous tank of a belly. Muscles soft and drooping from sloth. A dissipated face that seemed permanently angry. Lecherous —never mind. His horns were small and sharp and polished to a glow.

He waited until I reached bottom. "That's better. Now what kept you? It's been a good century since anyone called up a demon."

"They've forgotten how," I told him. "Nowadays everyone thinks you're supposed to draw the pentagram on the floor."

"The floor? They expect me to show up lying on my *back?*" His voice was thick with rage.

I shivered. My bright idea. A pentagram was a prison for demons. Why? I'd thought of the five points of a pentagram, and the five points of a spread-eagled man . . .

"Well?"

"I know, it doesn't make sense. Would you go away now, please?"

He stared. "You *have* forgotten a lot." Slowly and patiently, as to a child, he began to explain the implications of calling up a demon.

I listened. Fear and sick hopelessness rose in me until the concrete walls seemed to blur. "I am in peril of my immortal soul—" This was something I'd never considered, except academically. Now it was worse than that. To hear the demon talk, my soul was already lost. It had been lost since the moment I used the correct spell. I tried to hide my fear, but that was hopeless. With those enormous nostrils he must have smelled it.

He finished, and grinned as if inviting comment.

I said, "Let's go over that again. I only get one wish."

"Right."

"If you don't like the wish I've got to choose another."

"Right."

"That doesn't seem fair."

"Who said anything about fair?"

"—Or traditional. Why hasn't anyone heard about this deal before?"

"This is the standard deal, Jack. We used to give a better deal to some of the marks. The others didn't have time to talk because of that twenty-four-hour clause. If they wrote anything down we'd alter it. We have power over written things which mention us."

"That twenty-four-hour clause. If I haven't taken my wish in twenty-four hours, you'll leave the pentagram and take my soul anyway?"

"That's right."

"And if I do use the wish, you have to remain in the pentagram until my wish is granted, or until twenty-four hours are up. Then you teleport to Hell to report same, and come back for me immediately, reappearing in the pentagram."

"I guess teleport's a good word. I vanish and reappear. Are you getting bright ideas?"

"Like what?"

"I'll make it easy on you. If you erase the pentagram I can appear anywhere. You can erase it and draw it again somewhere else, and I've got to appear inside it."

A question hovered on my tongue. I swallowed it and asked another. "Suppose I wished for immortality?"

"You'd be immortal for what's left of your twenty-four hours." He grinned. His teeth were coal black. "Better hurry. Time's running out."

Time, I thought. Okay. All or nothing.

"Here's my wish. Stop time from passing outside of me."

"Easy enough. Look at your watch."

I didn't want to take my eyes off him, but he just exposed his black teeth again. So—I looked down.

There was a red mark opposite the minute hand on my Rolex. And a black mark opposite the hour hand.

The demon was still there when I looked up, still spread-eagled against the wall, still wearing that knowing grin. I moved around him, waved my hand before his face. When I touched him he felt like marble.

Time had stopped, but the demon had remained. I felt sick with relief.

The second hand on my watch was still moving. I had expected nothing less. Time had stopped for me —for twenty-four hours of interior time. If it had been exterior time I'd have been safe—but of course that was too easy.

I'd thought my way into this mess. I should be able to think my way out, shouldn't I?

I erased the pentagram from the wall, scrubbing until every trace was gone. Then I drew a new one, using a flexible metal tape to get the lines as straight as possible, making it as large as I could get it in the confined space. It was still only two feet across.

I left the basement.

I knew where the nearby churches were, though I hadn't been to one in too long. My car wouldn't start. Neither would my roommate's motorcycle. The spell which enclosed me wasn't big enough. I walked to a Mormon temple three blocks away.

The night was cool and balmy and lovely. City lights blanked out the stars, but there was a fine werewolf's moon hanging way above the empty lot where the Mormon temple should have been.

I walked another eight blocks to find the B'nai B'rith Synagogue and the All Saints Church. All I got out of it was exercise. I found empty lots. For me, places of worship didn't exist.

I prayed. I didn't believe it would work, but I prayed. If I wasn't heard was it because I didn't expect to be? But I was beginning to feel that the demon had thought of everything, long ago.

What I did with the rest of that long night isn't important. Even to me it didn't feel important. Twenty-four hours, against eternity? I wrote a fast outline on my experiment in demon raising, then tore it up. The demons would only change it. Which meant that my thesis was shot to hell, whatever happened. I carried a real but rigid Scotch terrier into Professor Pauling's room and posed it on his desk. The old tyrant would get a surprise when he looked up. But I spent most of the night outside, walking, looking my last on the world. Once I reached into a police car and flipped the siren on, thought about it, and flipped it off again. Twice I dropped into restaurants and ate someone's order, leaving money which I wouldn't need, paper-clipped to notes which read "The Shadow Strikes."

The hour hand had circled my watch twice. I got back to the basement at twelve ten, with the long hand five minutes from brenschluss.

That hand seemed painted to the face as I waited. My candles had left a peculiar odor in the basement, an odor overlaid with the stink of demon and the stink of fear. The demon hovered against the wall, no longer in a pentagram, trapped halfway through a wide-armed leap of triumph.

I had an awful thought.

Why had I believed the demon? Everything he'd said might have been a lie. And probably was! I'd been tricked into accepting a gift from the devil! I stood up, thinking furiously—I'd already accepted the gift, but—

The demon glanced to the side and grinned wider when he saw the chalk lines gone. He nodded at me, said, "Back in a flash," and was gone.

I waited. I'd thought my way into this, but—

A cheery bass voice spoke out of the air. "I knew you'd move the pentagram. Made it too small for me, didn't you? Tsk, tsk. Couldn't you guess I'd change my size?"

There were rustlings, and a shimmering in the air. "I know it's here somewhere. I can feel it. Ah."

He was back, spread-eagled before me, two feet tall and three feet off the ground. His black know-it-all grin disappeared when he saw the pentagram wasn't there. Then—he was seven inches tall, eyes bugged in surprise, yelling in a contralto voice. "Whereinhell's the—"

He was two inches of bright red toy soldier. "—Pentagram?" he squealed.

I'd won. Tomorrow I'd get to a church. If necessary, have somebody lead me in blindfold.

He was a small red star.

A buzzing red housefly.

Gone.

It's odd, how quickly you can get religion. Let one demon tell you you're damned . . . Could I really get into a church? Somehow I was sure I'd make it. I'd gotten this far; I'd outthought a demon.

Eventually he'd look down and see the pentagram. Part of it was in plain sight. But it wouldn't help him. Spread-eagled like that, he couldn't reach it to wipe it away. He was trapped for eternity, shrinking toward the infinitesimal but doomed never to reach it, forever trying to appear inside a pentagram which was forever too small. I had drawn it on his bulging belly.

The Deadlier
Weapon

HE was standing just off Overland Drive, at the mouth of the on ramp to the Santa Monica Freeway, eastbound. He waited with an air of ready confidence, and his thumbsmanship seemed practiced. His placement was perfect. A few yards further up the ramp, and no car could have stopped for him without being hit by the car behind. A few yards closer, and no driver would have known which route he wanted: the freeway, or the street going past the ramp.

That was what caught my attention: the perfect placement, not too far, not too near. A traveler, for sure. I dropped my arm out the window to signal, hit the brakes, and pulled up an easy foot and a half beyond him.

He was running before the car stopped. I pulled the lock knob and he threw the door open and was in, grinning, wasting no time. Good again. Nobody waits for a lazy hitchhiker; you trot or you don't ride. As soon as he was in I swung between two cars and headed up the ramp, accelerating.

The traffic wasn't bad, not at three in the afternoon. Still, when you enter a freeway you concentrate on the traffic. Everything else gets ignored. I hardly knew what my passenger looked like; I'd seen only a poised silhouette with its thumb raised against the afternoon sky. But I gave him points again. He didn't speak until I was firmly settled in the middle-right lane and could afford to relax a little.

I don't pick up riders often. When I do, I follow the whim of the moment. The ones who look chatty when I want peace and quiet, and the ones who look glum or taciturn when I'm after conversation—these get left standing. I like the unusual ones, the ones who seem to have a kind of salesmanship.

Six months ago there'd been a college girl on Wilshire, carrying a bright red Christmas package almost as big as she was. She was homesick for Kansas. She'd told me what freezing rains are like, when water falls from the sky at night and freezes where it hits, so that in the morning all the trees and bushes are tinkling crystal, crackling in the wind. That would be something to see. But I expect I never will.

Once there'd been a Negro on the freeway, carrying a gas can and smoking. As soon as he was in the car he'd tipped the ash off his cigarette into the gas can. "Okay," I'd said, to prove I was alert. "So you didn't run out of gas. Where you heading?"

"San Francisco," he'd told me. He'd started in Louisiana.

There was the guy who did run out of gas, stranded on the left of the freeway with his wife and four kids. "Oh, the kids are no trouble on a trip," he'd told me. "We know how to keep them interested. We play a game. The first kid to spot an Edsel gets a double ice-cream cone, immediately."

"Must make for frequent stops."

"How long since you last saw an Edsel?"

Right. I'd never seen two in the same day.

The hitchhiker said, "Thanks for the lift."

Traffic was fast and easy, the cars evenly spaced. I risked a look to the side.

He was young, somewhere in his mid-twenties. His nose was a touch too large and a touch too pointed, and his brown hair a touch too long. Gray plastic sunglasses, dark blue windbreaker over a white shirt, serviceable gray slacks. Shoes which looked rugged enough but which were not hiking shoes. He'd shaved recently. Despite the long hair, he looked too neat to have been on the road long. Perhaps he was just starting a trip.

"That's okay," I said. "You've used that thumb a lot, haven't you?"

"That's true." I heard a click then, but it didn't register until later. His voice was college educated, with a little too much tenor.

"How far you going this time?"

"Just far enough."

An odd answer. I glanced over at him and found the point of a knife just touching my larynx. "Watch the road," he said.

I turned back. Now I remembered the click. The knife was a switchblade with a six-inch blade, not very clean, but sharp, with the marks of a whetstone along the edge. I'd caught all of that in one glance.

"Neither of us is going to get hurt," the man with the knife said soothingly. He held the point at the side of my neck, just touching. "When you get the chance, you're going to pull over to the side, and I'm going to take your watch and the money in your wallet. Nothing else. I'll leave the wallet. I don't want your credit cards."

The lane to my left was clear. "Imagine how relieved I must be to hear it," I said, and eased over

My passenger pushed gently with the knife point. "Wrong direction," he told me. "You want to go right."

I shifted into the far left lane, a little too fast. The knife point was an itch over my carotid artery. My hands wanted to scratch it, and I had to fight to keep them on the wheel. "You've done this before," I said, keeping my voice light.

"What makes you think so?"

"Your wording seems too practiced. On the one hand, the knife. On the other, you've told me just what you'll take, and you'll leave me the rest. The other cars will be going too fast to notice us, right?"

"That's right." He'd kept his voice soft and slow while making his pitch, but now an edge crept in. "This isn't rush hour. Even if someone notices something, he'll be a mile past us before he decides to stop and do something about it. Now——" He put on a touch more pressure, and the itch became a burn. "Move over."

"Don't do that," I said. At the increase in pressure I'd turned to look him full in the face. He set his jaw and held the stare, and the knife was still at my throat. Except for that, and one other thing, it would have been a comic scene: two grown men trying to outstare each other.

"Watch the road," he said, not soothingly. And then, "I said watch the road. Dammit, watch the damn road!"

Suddenly he turned and braced himself against the padded dash with both hands. I looked forward, hit the brake and swerved. A navy blue Riviera missed us by a foot and dropped behind, weaving, the driver shouting soundlessly and leaning on his horn.

"Keep that knife out of my neck," I said. Some of the itch remained, and I reached up to scratch it. For my trouble I got a sharp stab of pain, and a film of blood on my fingertips. "And you can tell me something else. How do I know you won't kill me before you take my wallet?"

"Cooperate and you won't get hurt."

"Why not?"

He lost patience. With a smooth, quick motion, too fast for me to grab at his arm even if I wanted to, he had the knife tip at my neck. "Now pull over. Yeee!" He jerked back as if he'd touched something red hot.

Because I'd been less quick, but I didn't have as far to move. At the touch of the knife I'd yanked the wheel sixty degrees left and instantly back again. I pulled the car out of the emergency lane at the left of the freeway, fighting the drag of the gravel.

"Don't do that," I told him.

"What's *with* you?"

"Just in a bad mood, I guess."

He was backed up against the right front door of the Cadillac. He held the knife at ready, as if he were the defender and I the attacker. He licked his lips and asked, "Do you always drive this way when you're in a bad mood?"

"I've never been in this bad a mood before." I was trying to sound neither frightened nor belligerent. My smile must have looked peculiar, twisted, as if I'd put it on wrong.

"Look, all I want is your—"

"Shut up."

"You can keep your watch."

"Imagine my gratitude. Now will you shut up? You've got nothing to do with this."

"I—" He couldn't speak; he was half strangling on his own indignation. And I saw the overpass ahead, and I came alert, more than alert.

I'd passed here before, ignoring the scenery. Now I peered forward to get details. Some major highway crossed the freeway here. The overpass rose gently up a landscaped slope, leaped across eight lancs of empty space, and dropped as gently back. Halfway across the gap, between the eastbound and westbound lanes, were massive concrete pillars. Ramps curved out to join freeway with highway, and there were green signs to tell what turnoff this was, if I'd cared.

"What's wrong?" my passenger said edgily, and I realized how rigidly I was sitting and how hard I was gripping the wheel. I didn't relax. "See that bridge?"

"Sure."

"Okay."

"What about it?"

"Nothing." I wasn't even trying to smile now.

"All I want is some cash," the hitchhiker explained patiently. "You pull over to the side and stop, and—"

"And you cut my throat and take the car too. The cops get nothing but a missing-person report."

"No, no, no. Honest. All I want—"

"I don't care what you want."

"What do *you* want? Do you want to live?" Amazing, how his voice had lost those soothing overtones.

I didn't answer. The overpass was closer.

The hitchhiker clamped his lips together, nerving himself to something. Suddenly, snakelike, he reached with the knife. I jerked the wheel, and he pulled back against the door. The wheel damn near jerked out of my hands as we hit gravel. To make it worse, the freeway was curving right. I fought us around, and the bridge was almost on us.

There were no cars near me. Maybe they didn't like the way I drove.

Still the freeway curved right, gently as always. I didn't curve with it. I had the accelerator on the floor, and we went faster and faster, the hitchhiker and the Cadillac and me, edging over onto the gravel. Up ahead, the gravel safety lane ended, and there was the concrete supporting pillar of the bridge, with two red-faceted reflectors shining in the midafternoon sunlight.

I aimed the car right at the reflectors.

My passenger seemed frozen. Only his head moved, swiveling to look at the supporting pillar and then back to my face and then to the pillar and back to me. The pillar was coming up like a cream-colored wall. I was terrified. I made no attempt to hide it. Considering the way the wheel was jumping, trying to pull across the gravel and into the divider fence before we could reach the bridge support, I must have looked like a man wrestling an alligator. There was sweat in my eyes, and at the last moment I whipped the edge of my right hand across my forehead and back to the wheel. Now my hand was dripping wet.

The concrete came at me.

I whipped the wheel hard over, putting my whole body into it. The car slewed, tried to move sideways, tried to roll over. We were going to hit sideways, through the fragile guard rail and into the supporting pillar. Then, with utmost reluctance, the car moved skidding to the right. Suddenly the concrete was behind us. My passenger made a high, whimpering sound.

"Hesitation marks," I gasped. I couldn't get enough air. Reality was a blur. Was I about to faint? I certainly didn't want to faint.

"You're crazy. Crazy!"

I fumbled for a cigarette and managed to get it to my mouth. "There's always hesitation marks. A man shoots himself in the head, you find holes in the wall where he jerked the gun away the first four times. If he cuts his throat you find three or four slashes where he didn't cut deep enough." I was gasping out the words, fighting for air. I had to have air.

"You're out of your mind."

"The thing is, if I have to die, I might as well pick the way I want to go. Right?"

"What are you talking about?"

"I was going to marry a girl."

"Congratulations." If my passenger was trying for sarcasm, it didn't come through. He only sounded scared. He sat facing straight toward me, with one leg on the seat and his back hard up against the door, watching.

"Thanks. Thanks a whole hell of a lot. Only she decided I wasn't her type. She—she tried to tell me we'd both known it all along. We'd just been fooling ourselves, she said. Liar."

"They do that," said my passenger.

"Everybody does that. You know how my dad told me he and Mom were getting divorced?" My cigarette was still in my mouth, unlit. I reached and stabbed at the car lighter. "I was fifteen. They called me into the living room and—"

"I don't *care* what your father told you when you were fifteen!"

"I do. My dad walked a few times around the room and then finally he said, 'I suppose you know your mother and I are separated.' Liar. They'd kept it from me because they thought it might interfere with my finals at school."

All I saw of him, I saw with the corner of my eye. But I saw him start to say something, stop, close his eyes tight to think.

The lighter popped out.

He blurted, "You're *crazy!* You can't *kill* yourself just because some bitch gives you the shaft!"

I pulled the lighter out and reached across the seat to touch it to the tip of his nose. He never moved to stop me. He couldn't believe what I was doing, not until he actually felt the heat. Then he screamed and threw his arms over his face. He missed grabbing my arm because I'd already pulled it back and was lighting my cigarette.

"She's not a bitch," I told him. "And if she was, you wouldn't be the one to say it. Keep your dirty mouth off her."

"Let me off," said the hitchhiker. He'd forgotten he had the knife. He'd tried it before and it hadn't worked.

"Why should I?"

"I never tried to kill you. It's not fair."

"Who said anything about fair?" My grin felt natural now. After all, we were even. The blood on my neck matched the burn on his nose.

"Look, you don't want to kill yourself. You don't want to die. You're just kidding yourself. Just wait. Just wait until tomorrow. You'll feel different, really you will. I've felt like that myself, I really have but it always went away, sometimes it lasted for days but it always—"

"It's too late."

"It's not too late! You're still alive!"

"This isn't my car."

"What?"

"Do I look like a Cadillac driver?"

Eyes see what they're trained to see, what they expect to see. A polo shirt is just a T-shirt with a collar, except for the material. Pants are pants, except to the guy who wears them. He knows if they bind, or if they're too loose, or if they're tailored to fit just right.

If the seat looks shiny, then they're too old, but how can you tell when he's sitting down?

"You stole it," he said.

I bobbed my head a couple of times, jerkily.

"Let me out."

"I don't want to get knifed."

"Please."

"Fasten your seat belt."

"Why?" But he knew. He knew.

"We're going to have an accident."

"Let me out first. Look, I—will you please look?"

I found I was strangling the wheel again. Because up ahead was where the freeway became a bowl of concrete noodles. I'd driven this route before. Here in downtown Los Angeles was where the Santa Monica Freeway led into the Harbor, Santa Ana, and San Bernardino Freeways. The ramps led up and over and around and under each other, and most of the time there was nothing but empty space to left and right. Speeding cars and empty space, separated by fragile metal rails and common sense.

My passenger knew it too. He was swiveling his head, toward the road, toward me, toward the road, toward me. Then he snapped out of it. He yelled, "Will you *look at me?*"

I looked, and he twitched, because now I wasn't watching the road. He was holding the knife out the window, holding it with two fingers around the tip of the handle. He let it drop, ostentatiously, and I saw it bounce once in the mirror. "I dropped the knife," he said. "You saw it. Now let me out."

I nodded. I braked and swung to the left. The car lurched and jerked and tried to pull free and slowed and stopped, not too far from where there wouldn't have been gravel to stop on. Cars whizzed past, and the wind of their passing sounded like blows against the side of the Cadillac.

"Out."

"Not here! I'll be killed!"

I touched the accelerator and the car jumped forward. He was out and around the side and behind the trunk in one smooth, lithe motion, and if there'd been a car coming it would have hit him. I touched the accelerator again to get beyond him, then reached across to slam the door he'd left open.

At the next gap in the traffic I was off, accelerating hard to keep from being hit from behind. The last I saw of the hitchhiker, he was hunched over the guard rail, actually using it for support, not looking at the four lanes of traffic he'd have to pass alive.

I edged to the right across four lanes of hurtling cars, being careful. I saw no point in getting killed now. I took the next turnoff, slowing, feeling my hands begin to shake. My cigarette was still going, and I dragged on it, practically breathing through it. Amazingly, it was mostly unburned. I turned in at the first gas station I saw, stopped alongside the pumps, and rested my head on the wheel. I rubbed my forehead against the smooth surface, harder and harder, because the sensation told me I was still alive.

"What can we do for you? I said—hey. Mister, are you all right?"

"I'm fine. Where's a telephone?"

"Over there." They were in plain sight. I couldn't have missed them if I'd bothered to look first.

"Good. Fill it up. I've got to call the police."

I had trouble getting the coin in the slot.

"About his height," I told the desk sergeant. "Five eleven, say. You wouldn't call him skinny, but he's not fat. Brown hair, a little too long, parted on the left. Long, thin face. By the time you get to him he should have a great big blister on the end of his nose."

"Why?"

"At one point I touched him there with a cigarette lighter."

"You did!" Hah! I'd surprised him. At first he'd sounded like someone who could never be surprised by anything. "Go on, Mr. Ruch."

"He's wearing dark glasses, a dark blue windbreaker, gray slacks. I left him stranded on the wrong side of the eastbound lane, just west of the Olympic turnoff."

"We'll find him, Mr. Ruch. Can you come down to the station and give us a signed statement?" He told me how to get there.

"Okay, fine, but will you give me an hour and a half? I need a drink."

"I can believe that. No hurry, Mr. Ruch. But we do need that statement."

One fast drink stopped my shakes, at least on the outside. I thought I could trust my voice now, so I called Carla in Garden Grove. "I've had some car trouble, honey. Nothing expensive, but I won't be home for dinner. Tell Stan and Eva I'm sorry, and I'll be in around eight if I'm lucky."

"Oh, that's a shame. What kind of trouble?"

"Tell you later."

"You have to get up early tomorrow, remember? Rehearsal."

"No problem. I'll be home in plenty of time."

By the time I got home I'd know how to tell Carla the truth in a way that wouldn't scare the pants off her.

Two drinks and I began to giggle, thinking about the blister on the end of the hitchhiker's nose, thinking about the hopeful look on his face when he dropped the knife out the window, how he had to make so *damn* sure I was watching him. Giggles was too much of a good thing, so I had a sandwich and a glass of milk to drown the second drink.

. . . I could legitimately tell Carla that the hitchhiker had never had a chance. It would reassure her, and it was true. I'd been better armed from the beginning. He'd had nothing but a knife. I had had a car. Much deadlier.

I reached the station half an hour late. They'd changed desk men. I was explaining why I was there when they brought in the hitchhiker.

He wasn't struggling. He seemed completely exhausted. He actually had trouble walking. But his head came up when he saw me. The tip of his nose was a small white bubble surrounded by angry red flesh.

"So you didn't have the guts!" he snarled. "You chickened out! You yellow-bellied—" He paused to think up an adequately insulting noun, ignoring the police officer who jerked warningly at his arm.

"I couldn't go through with it," I admitted, and looked sheepishly down at the toes of my shoes. Why tell him? He had enough troubles.

———————

The preceding story was *not* autobiographical. I daydreamed it while driving the Santa Monica Freeway.

The guy who asked me that question tells me that he was once threatened by a hitchhiker with a knife . . . and that a friend of his tells the same story. Neither of the two tried that fancy suicide approach. They explained to their assailants that if they didn't see total surrender damn quick, they were going to obliterate the right side of the car against a tree at sixty mph. The left side of the car would have to take its chances.

It worked for them. I hope I won't ever have to try that approach myself.

The
Nonesuch

The newer stories begin here.
Not everything I do is entirely original. The plot
for the following story was stolen. You will probably
recognize the source.

THERE was one breed of predator on Haven, and it
covered that world. If ever there had been other predators, they must have died out long ago, unable to
compete. No predator of Earth—wolf, hyena, lion—
could have matched a killer who could read the minds
of its prey.

The first generation of men on Haven had lived
behind electrified barbed wire, with electrified double
gates arranged in pairs, airlock fashion. The predators
never tried to break through the barrier, and they
never missed a man who ventured beyond. Large
armed groups usually returned with members missing,
and the survivors had never seen a thing.

Haven was a lush green world, but the Haven colony seemed doomed. How could men conquer a world
from behind barbed wire?

Thirty years of that; and then a defense was found.

Afterward it was as if there were no predators at
all on Haven. The colony bloomed. But the first set-

tlers still tended to stay within the city; and the tale of the *nonesuch* remained.

The nonesuch was stalking a young girl.

He had not caught sight or smell of her. But, beyond a rise of rolling green hill, he had touched her mind. Her rather pleasant thoughts trickled through his brain, and he moved toward her.

The nonesuch was lazy by inclination. He rarely had trouble keeping himself fed. The prey never ran, not if he was careful. And the girl seemed in no hurry.

The nonesuch didn't hurry either. He plodded upward, toward the crest of the hill.

Starbase Town was well behind her. Doris Mac-Aran strolled through a dwarf forest, smiling as she sniffed the smells of growing vegetation. Alien smells, but not to her. She wore a backpack and canteen. The eggs and sugar and flour and ham in her backpack were for old Hildegarde Burns, Great-Aunt Hildegarde who couldn't come to town herself because she'd sprained an ankle. And Great-Uncle Horace was at a silver-mining site far east of here . . . but who would need an excuse to go hiking on a day like this?

Doris MacAran. Sixteen years old, black-haired, darkly tanned, healthy, active, uncommonly pretty. Her health was a matter of selection, derived from eight great-grandparents who had been chosen to colonize a world. Active: well, on a colony world everyone walked. The vehicle industry was rolling along, but what it built was VTOL craft to explore the further reaches of the continent.

She ate as she walked: nuts and sugar-coated puffed wheat, an adequate trail snack. Dry gray bushes gave off a spicy smell as she brushed by them. She passed spear trees, slender vertical shafts of red wood, each with an artificial-looking ball of green leaves at the point. Sometimes she angled her path to cross a patch of mattress plant. Mattress plant was like thick-piled green cotton with roots, one plant sometimes covering an acre of ground, delightful to walk on. It was all familiar, part of her world.

She kept a rhythmic pace, placing her feet almost heel-to-toe in a walk that moved the mass of her backpack straight forward instead of bouncing it up and down. In an hour she'd be in sight of the Burns' house, and no trouble finding it. People who lived this far from Starbase Town usually preferred hilltops.

The nonesuch paused at the crest of the hill. He looked; he sniffed. Sight and smell were none too sharp in a nonesuch, and the girl was too far downslope. But her thoughts were clear and bright. Her brain was larger and more intelligent than any native to this world, excepting that of another nonesuch. Intelligence was a liability on Haven. A large brain, clear thoughts, made it easy for a nonesuch to follow.

The nonesuch was not a local. He had wandered into this area, following a rich concentration of the thoughts of meat. The locals were few, and none had challenged him for territory. He was big, his claws were sharp, he could fight.

The locals were few. That was peculiar, with thousands of human minds clustered a few miles distant, and thousands more scattered throughout the region, all broadcasting clear, bright thoughts. The locals left the humans strictly alone. They were numerous and easy to follow, but a local nonesuch would not prey on them. Why not?

He would learn.

The nonesuch knew from her thoughts that the girl had not seen him, was not looking toward him. He started down the hill.

Slender spear trees, low gray bushes, patches of mattress plant. Nothing big could hide in such cover. Then what was it Doris had seen moving on the side of that big hill? There were no big animals in this region of Haven, except for domestic sheep and cattle

. . . and perhaps a nonesuch or two, Doris thought, smiling at herself.

Motion near the hill's green crest. She'd looked again and it hadn't been there. A cloud shadow? Or another hiker? Perhaps she'd have company when she finished her walk.

Pity Mark hadn't been able to join her. She toyed with a daydream: he'd finished early—the computer he had to fix had been unplugged or something—and he had followed her. Without a backpack he could double her pace.

Or it was a nonesuch. But no, she could do without such company!

The nonesuch: she'd heard about it as a child. *Don't go outside the city without an adult, Little Doris. The nonesuch will get you. You'll never know it's there, because it's always behind you.*

Why, Dad?

Because it's so ugly, Little Doris. It won't let you see it. It's ashamed of the way it looks.

She smiled, remembering how solemnly she'd listened. And there had been stories of bad little girls eaten by the nonesuch . . . Of course that had been a long time ago . . .

The nonesuch had fallen flat and frozen when he sensed the girl looking toward him, Now, as she resumed her rhythmic stride, he began moving again. But he was disturbed.

The picture in the girl's mind was very like a nonesuch.

It stood upright on its hind legs, on broad flat feet. Its head was round, its neck virtually nonexistent. Its eyes were tiny and close-set. Its teeth were large and triangular, and two large fangs protruded over the lower lip in front. Its skin was smooth, mottled in two shades of greenish brown. Brown hair flopped forward from the crown of its head. Its hands were big, like a man's with both thumbs missing, and each finger was tipped with a crescent claw.

It was not quite a nonesuch, this picture in the girl's mind; some of the features were humanized. But it was close. She should have been frightened, but what he felt in her was certainly not fright.

The nonesuch was wary. He would follow his habit. He would not let himself be seen.

. . . a long time ago. Dad and his nonesuch! And her uncles were in on it too. She was six before she caught on.

It's always behind me, is it, Dad? Then I'll never know if it's real or not, will I? But how do you know what it looks like, Dad, if nobody's ever seen one?

And finally Dad and Uncle Ray had laughed and given in. The nonesuch was like Santa Claus: a story. Adults thought it was fun to tell stories to kids. For a year or so afterward she'd wondered if Earth was another such tall story. But Earth was real; there were pictures, there were infrequent starships . . .

The nonesuch had a problem. It had run across a grazer.

The small quick beast was closer than the girl. It was moving round and round the borders of a mattress plant, trimming the borders with blunt teeth. The nonesuch sensed its placid thoughts, its continuous dull hunger and its continuous chewing. It hadn't seen him yet.

The nonesuch was torn. He could have been on the grazer in a few minutes. The grazer would make a full meal . . . but at the last moment it was bound to make some disturbance, and the girl would turn and see him.

With some regret the nonesuch moved on. He sensed the animal's sudden start as it saw him, then fear and frantic haste, dwindling with distance.

It was curiosity that moved the nonesuch after the more difficult prize. Partly it was: *how will human meat taste?* and partly: *why do the others leave these beasts alone?* One question might answer another.

Human meat might be poisonous, or merely unpalatable. But no local nonesuch had told him so.

In fact, they would not answer him at all on this subject.

And partly it was: *She knows of me, but she doesn't believe in me. Incomprehension.* Something alien here, something that went with the girl's quiet conviction that she had come from a different world.

She was thinking of a man now . . . a man somewhat older than she, who had not proposed sex to her but who might . . . and her imagination was working in all her senses. The nonesuch savored sensations sharper than his own even in imagination: sight and touch and somasthesia. He liked the girl's mind.

He would have liked to talk to her.

Why not? She was not a nonesuch . . . she was very alien . . . but surely there must be concepts basic to all life. The nonesuch thought it through, then projected the most universal message he knew:

I'M GOING TO EAT YOU

There! She had reacted, a tensing of viscera, her head turning to look behind her, a shiver . . . but now she had forgotten. He had not truly reached her mind. She lacked that sense entirely, like an animal. Pity.

Instead he savored in anticipation her sudden sharp knowledge, there at the end, when she would realize the reality of the nonesuch. How would it feel to her? To him? He increased his pace.

She looked back as she passed a barrel tree. For an instant she was *sure* there was something behind her. She almost went back to look. Then one of the pig-sized grazing beasts went bounding past her as if death itself were at its heels, and she went on, laughing. When they put those oversized hind legs to the test the bounders always looked like they were trying to do somersaults.

She ought to be getting close to Great-Aunt Hildegarde's house. The pack was getting heavy.

And there was still that feeling of something *behind* her.

The barrel tree was a piece of luck. A nonesuch was big. He could never have fed himself had he not been unusually good at the predator business. A barrel tree was about the only growing thing big enough to hide a nonesuch. He kept the thick trunk and dark green crown between himself and the girl as he moved in for the kill.

When he reached the barrel tree the girl was twenty meters beyond. Close enough. A nonesuch was no good for a long chase, but for short sprints he could move like light itself.

Her back was to him.

He charged.

She heard something. She turned, awkwardly because of the pack.

She saw him.

It was just as Dad and Uncle Ray had described it. Tiny, close-set eyes; wide mouth with triangular buck teeth; floppy mop of brown hair; big hands with long nails; short legs and big clumsy feet. A vicious caricature of some yokel farmhand, and it was gallumping toward her with clawed hands outstretched in moronic lust.

Doris's eyes bugged. A giggle bubbled up into her throat and hung there. There *wasn't* any such thing. She *knew* that. Was she losing her mind? She closed her eyes hard, so tight it hurt, then opened them fast.

Sure enough, there was nothing there.

She looked about her, searching for the pattern of shadows that must have sparked that ridiculous illusion. A passing cloud shadow, perhaps? Nothing.

She'd been stupid; she'd gone too long without a rest break. Doris walked back to the only shade in sight—the barrel tree—dropped her pack against its trunk and sat down under the crown of dark green leaves.

It was the dull gnawing of hunger that brought him back to himself. Had he been asleep? Asleep, standing up?

Memory came joltingly. The nonesuch mewled and began patting himself with his hands. Yes, he could feel that. *That* was real.

He had not been asleep. The nonesuch knew what sleep felt like. He had been—gone. Now he was back (he felt his face; the claws pricked his skin), he was back, yes. From where?

From nothing.

She'd looked at him and not believed. Looked at him and seen—illusion, a trick of the mind, a trick of light and shadow. She'd convinced him in that moment, and there had been telepathic feedback, and—he was gone. Gone, until hunger made him real again.

There was a grazer nearby, wandering toward him around the curve of a mattress plant. He plodded toward it, reluctantly, prodded by sharp hunger. The girl was nowhere near. He must have been gone for a long time.

The grazer hadn't seen him yet.

Suppose it refused to believe in him?

Singularities
Make Me
Nervous

HOMECOMING. The vast interstellar spaces have brought me back to my starting point, there below me, at the top of Rand's Needle. Three hundred stories of glass windows flash sunset fire at me, and the taxi slants down toward the landing roof.

Homecoming. I should be feeling safe and warm. I do not.

A broad flight of black marble steps leads me down into the lobby. I hail the guard before he notices me. "Hello, Emilio—"

He smiles. "Good morning, Mister Cox." He waits while I use the key—he doesn't have one himself—then holds the elevator door for me. He's noticed nothing unusual.

I hold my apartment key ready. Will he have visitors? But that's silly. I *didn't* have visitors that night.

Twelve floors down. I stand squarely in front of the peephole and ring the bell. A voice I know asks, "Who is it?"

"Can you see me?"

"Yes."

I grin. My face feels tight. My breathing is funny. "Who am I, then?"

Hesitation. "I wish I could take your retina prints."

"They'd match, George. I'm you."

"Sure you are."

He's skeptical. I am not offended. "I'm *you*. And I've got a key to my own apartment. Shall I prove it?"

"Go ahead."

I unlock the door and walk in. The shock of recognition gets me in the pit of the stomach. Tables, chairs, favorite recline chair, couch showing the barely visible stain of a spilled eggnog. The Eddie Jones originals. The gallon brandy bottle on the wet bar. Twenty-six years in space, most of it in frozen sleep, but now it's over. I'm home.

It's all here, all in place, right down to the tenant, George Cox, who is standing well back from me, taking no chances. He's holding an enormous folding knife with an engraved blade like a broad silver leaf. I say, "I can tell you where you got that."

"So can a lot of my friends." He doesn't relax.

"I didn't expect this to be easy. George, do you remember when you were, oh, eighteen or so? Going to Cal Tech. One night you got so lonely and so horny you called a girl you'd only met once in your life, at one of Glenda's birthday parties. She was a little plump and very sexy, remember? You called her but you got her parents. You were so nervous and embarrassed that—"

"Shut *up*. All right, I remember. What was her name?"

I can't remember. I tell him so.

"Right again," he says.

"Okay. Remember that Kansas sunset where the whole sky was split down the middle by one dark blue beam? You could follow it up across the sky and down into the east, almost to the horizon."

"Yah. Unbelievable. I never saw it happen again." He considers, then folds the knife and drops it in a drawer. "You're me. How about a drink?"

"What do you think? Shall I mix?"

"I'll do it," he says.

I let him. I don't want to infringe on his territorial

instincts. He goes to the trouble of mixing Navy Grogs
—a compliment: he's decided it's a special occasion.
I don't remember that detail from the night that I was
him. I cut the straws while he's at work, and he gives
me a sharp look. Nobody else would have known to
do that.

"You're me," he says, when we've settled in chairs
and have imbibed some of the life-giving fluid. "How?"

"The black hole. Bauerhaus Four."

"Ah." He was expecting that. "So I made it back.
They haven't even picked me to go yet."

"They will."

He sips at his drink and waits.

"Black holes," I say. "Singularities. Stars that have
collapsed all the way to a point. They've been there in
the general theory of relativity for a hundred years or
more. The first black hole was found in nineteen
seventy-two, in Cygnus, circling a puffy yellow-giant
star. But Bauerhaus Four is a lot closer."

He nods. He's heard it before, a couple of weeks
ago by his own reckoning, when Doctor Kurt Bauerhaus himself came to lecture us at the Spacebranch
Authority Training Center.

"But," I tell him, "not even Doctor Bauerhaus wants
to talk about what goes on inside the Schwarzschild
radius of a black hole. Singularities upset people like
Bauerhaus."

"It's time travel that does that."

"I don't think so. Forget the time travel aspect and
look at a black hole. A mass so big that when it
collapses it goes all the way to a point. Even light red-
shifts to zero before it can get out. Would you believe
it?"

He shrugs. "It's in the equations. Bauerhaus said
so. Relativity's peculiar from square one, and it's
checked out every time it's been tested."

"A hole into another universe, maybe, or into another part of this one, maybe. That's in the equations
too. And there's a path around a rotating black hole
that brings you back to your starting point without

even going through the singularity. Which sounds harmless enough until you realize you're talking about event-points—points in space time."

He raises his glass. "Skoal."

I raise mine. "Right. I'm back before I started the trip Most astrophysicists would rather believe there's a hole in the theory. Singularities make them nervous."

"Time travel makes *me* nervous."

"You can see for yourself." I rap my chest. "It's safe."

He doesn't look nervous. We're both relaxing now under the influence of the drinks. It's been a long, weary time since I tasted the cold brown sweet power of a Navy Grog.

He says, "I'm only supposed to circle it, you know. And drop the probes."

"I know. But *Ulysses*'s autopilot is built to send one of the probes on a round trip through the Schwarzschild radius of the star and back to its starting event-point. You just take *Ulysses* through that path instead of sending the probe. You can't go wrong. You go back in time about twenty-six years, which brings you back to the Moon six months early."

He shifts in his chair. "The Moon? Not Earth orbit?"

"Not yet. I've got *Ulysses* hidden on the back side of the Moon. From there I took a jet platform to within sight of Ley Crater, then hid that. I came back to Miami on a tourist shuttle. A year from now I'll go back to the Moon, pick up *Ulysses* and come home to a cheering mob."

"Six months after takeoff. That'll tell them you *did* go through the Schwarzschild radius. Bauerhaus Four is eleven light-years away."

"Well, you can make your own decision on that—"

"The hell. You're *me,* and you've already decided!"

"I've got a year to change my mind. But look at it this way. NASA is *entitled* to know you can use a black hole this way. They're paying for the trip. And what can they do to me?"

"Yeah—"

"And I'll be damned if I'll hide out for twenty-six years."

He nods. "Right. G-george—" He stumbles over our name. "Just what's the point of all this?"

He's guessed that already, I think. "Stocks. Luckily you're already playing the stock market a little. I've memorized the behavior of several stocks for the next six months. In six months we'll be a millionaire. Then we'll go through a stack of newspapers and *you'll* do the memorizing."

He grins. "What for? We'll already have the money."

"I hope you're putting me on," I say uneasily

He nods. I'm reassured, partly. But I'm the vulnerable one. If we make one mistake in the program, if the Typewriter of Time writes a different history this time around, *I'm* the one who'll disappear in a puff of smoke. Or will I? The paradoxes are all new, and we have to guess at how they'll work out.

I came back from the Moon under an assumed name: C. Cretemaster. As C. Cretemaster I now rent an apartment across town from the younger George Cox. I don't want to bug him overmuch with my presence.

I certainly bugged *me,* back when I was him. I was afraid the older George Cox would try to take over my life. He didn't . . . and yet he did. His very existence hemmed me in more than prison bars. I would make *these* choices, not those; where the road of life forked I would turn *this* way; all others were barred to me.

He's going through that now. I stay out of his way.

And I'm *still* going through it. I'm the older George Cox now, but it doesn't help. My life is planned out in the minutest detail. My free will—my illusion of free will—will not return to me until *Ulysses* disappears among the stars. I didn't expect this.

We meet rarely during the next five months. He and Frank Curey and Yoki Lee are deeply involved in astronaut training. I'm living off his salary, but that's okay with both of us, because the value of his stocks is building and building. I'm doing all the manipulating, in our name. He doesn't have time.

It's like playing poker with reader cards! I feel no guilt: only a vast elation. The stocks move as I command them . . . or vice versa. Last time through this I wondered why the money didn't increase even faster. Now that I'm handling it myself, I know. There's a limit to how fast you can move money around, even when you know exactly where it ought to go.

"I feel sorry for Yoki and Frank," he tells me. "They're working just as hard as I am, and for what?"

"Think of it as predestination," I tell him. I wish I could think of a better answer. I remember how disappointed they will be, and how bravely they will try to hide it.

The three of them spend two months in *Ulysses* itself. The ship is complete now; only the trainee pilots are not ready. I can see it up there at night, a splinter of light cruising slowly across the stars.

And I remember:

Passing the planets, passing through the cometary belt. Months of fiddling with the ram fields, adjusting the flow of interstellar hydrogen into the fusion region, until finally I was in clear space. Climbing into the cold-sleep tank.

Waking at midpoint, staring in awe at the way the stars had changed, blazing blue-white before me, glowing dull red behind; then turning to the tricky task of reversing the fields to channel the fusion blast forward.

Waking again to find that the stars were back to normal. Using the Forward Mass Indicator to seek out Bauerhaus Four. *There.* Searching that point with the telescope—and *nothing*.

Dropping Probes One and Two. Into the ergosphere,

the elliptical region of spin around the Schwarzschild radius. The size of the ergosphere would tell me how much of the star's spin the black hole had carried into itself: the dimensions of the path through the singularity.

One was circling the black hole hundreds of times a second before it disappeared. *Two* followed the same path, fired a jet before it reached the Schwarzschild radius, and shot away at just less than lightspeed.

I remember plotting the course for Probe Three.

Following it down.

Am I really going to do this foolish thing?

Hell, I've already done it.

I remember the way the stars blurred near that empty point. Once a star passed directly behind it, and for a moment it was a ring of light. There was no *bump* as I went through the Schwarzschild radius— only the gradually increasing pull of tidal force—but somehow I knew I had left the universe.

Free at last. Free of the older George Cox.

Sure I was.

"We've been moving money around for five months now," I tell him on his return, "and we've passed the million mark. How's it feel to be a millionaire?"

"Pretty good." He smiles in triumph as he looks through the books, but the smile is a bit forced when he turns to face me. He's not used to me yet.

"Okay. Now, your job." I hand him a stack of newspapers. "Memorize these stocks."

"*All* of them?"

"No, just the ones that're going to go up, and when. But I haven't marked them, George. You'll have to find and mark them and then memorize them."

He grumbles, as I did once. "You've had more free time than me."

"Haven't we got cause and effect screwed up enough? I get this nightmare feeling that if we louse up the natural laws any worse, I'll go out like a candle flame. Will you do this for the best friend you ever had? Please?"

He takes the newspapers.

I don't see him for a week.

One afternoon I answer a ringing telephone. It's him. His eyes are wide, his face is white. Before I can speak he blurts it out. "They picked Frank!"

"What? The hell they did. They picked *me*."

"They picked Frank! George, what'll we do?"

His voice is fading. There's a singing in my head. The room is fading, going blurry. My knees buckle, and I drift toward the floor. I want to scream, but I can't.

I'm cold. There is rough-textured rug under my chin. I feel it with my hands, and it's real, it's really there. I must have fainted.

The other George is yelling out of the phone. "George! *George!*" I manage to get my face in front of the camera. I tell him, "Sit tight. I'll be right over."

This time we aren't sitting. We're pacing, passing each other, talking in random directions . . . it would look like low comedy if anyone could see us

He's saying, "We could just forget it. Share the money. Ignore the paradox."

"I hate that thought. George, get it through your head that the paradox is *me*. If this time track doesn't go as it went, I'm gone! We've got to do *something*."

"Like what? Steal the ship?"

"Hum. That's—"

"If I steal *Ulysses*, you get court-martialed! *You!*"

"Hah! They wouldn't even look for me."

"And how are you going to spend our million dollars in my name?"

Dammit. He's right. The effort I've spent, the risks I've taken, all for nothing.

I stop in midstride. "Maybe they won't suspect me."

"Hah. You couldn't get onto the shuttle field without showing your face."

"Hah yourself. Someone must have been imperson-
ating me. I've got an alibi."

"Alibi?" He suddenly starts to laugh. "Hey, I'm
going to make drinks. This won't make any sense at
all to a sober man."

A month to wait. A month to make plans. But it
isn't: they've moved the take off date up two weeks.
I'm starting to lose faith in any kind of consistent
universe. At night I'm afraid to fall asleep. Every
morning comes as a joyful surprise. *I'm still here.*

I wish I could talk to Bauerhaus.

We braced him after the lecture. A small, round,
voluble man, he was willing to talk at any length about
cosmology in general. The Big Bang that may or may
not have started the universe, that may have sown
the universe with quantum black holes smaller than
an atomic nucleus and weighing more than a large
asteroid . . . the possibility that the universe itself is
inside somebody else's black hole . . . white holes
spewing matter from nowhere .

But they fought clear of one subject. "Gentlemen,
we simply do not know what goes on inside the
Schwarzschild radius of a black hole. We do not
know that the matter actually goes to a point. It may
be stopped by a force stronger than any we know of."

What of the paths through a rotating black hole?

He smiled like one sharing a joke. "We expect to
find a hole in the theory here. We postulate a Law of
Cosmic Censorship, a process that would prevent anything from ever leaving a black hole. Otherwise we
could get black holes with so much spin to them that
there is no Schwarzschild radius around the singularity. A naked singularity would be *very* messy. The
mathematics is inconsistent—like dividing zero by
zero."

If he could see me now, both of me together, surely
it would be singularity enough. We do not risk being
seen together. The younger George Cox continues his
training. Newsmen interview him and Yuri on the

need for more Bussard ramjets, scout ships to seek out Earthlike worlds circling other stars. The older George Cox plays the stock market, and waits.

Frank Curey has spent as much time in space as I have until the *Ulysses* flight, which hasn't happened yet. He stands about five feet zero, stocky and well muscled. His big square jaw gives him a bulldog look. He masses less than me or Yuri. So do the food and oxygen required to keep him alive for the year and a half he'll be awake.

There's no reason Spacebranch shouldn't have picked him over me; yet I keep wondering. What was different this time? Did the younger George concentrate too much on his stocks, too little on training? Did he stop trying, because I was the proof that he would succeed anyway?

Too late now. We've had one break. They picked me to pilot the ferry ship up and to help Frank with the final checkout of *Ulysses*.

Frank and I got through the check points together. The guards pass us through with no fuss. The shuttle field is bright with artificial lights beneath a gray-black sky.

Frank is nervous, excited. He's talking too much. Muscles flex at the edges of his jaw. "Twenty-six years. What can happen in twenty-six years? They could have immortality by then. Or a world dictatorship. Teleportation. Faster-than-light travel."

"They could get that from you, if Probe Three works out."

"Yeah. Yeah. If Probe Three comes back about the time I leave . . . but that's not too useful for space travel, George. There aren't enough black holes. No kidding, George, what d'you think I'll find when I come back?"

Yourself. It's on the tip of my tongue, but I swallow it. "Me, waiting at the shuttle field to tell you all about it. Unless you go too far in. Then you might not come out until every star is dead."

He clears his throat. "I know."

I say, "Care to change your mind?" Thinking there's a chance . . .

"Oh, come *on*," he snaps. That settles that.

We've almost reached the shuttle. It's a lifting body, not large, with a radiation shield around the tailpipe and an escalator ramp leading up into the nose. I'm talking too much myself; I'm as nervous as Frank. Lucky there were two gates. I half-expected the guards to stop us, on grounds that one of us was already inside . . . but apparently he got through without a hitch. Or else he didn't make it.

Frank is stepping onto the ramp when the other George Cox slides like a shadow from behind it. He's holding a heavy spanner.

And wiry Frank whips around and plants his fist in George's belly, crosses instantly with the right, plenty of class that boy shows. George goes down like a consignment of cooked spaghetti, flat on his back, his face turned up to the harsh lights.

Frank sees his face. He freezes.

I don't have a spanner. I use the stiff edge of my palm against Frank's neck. Frank turns, looking bewildered, and I hit him on the point of the jaw. He goes down.

I take his pulse. It hasn't stopped.

George Cox's heart is beating too, but he's showing no other sign of life. I don't need to take my own pulse; it's thundering in my ears. The other George Cox may need a hospital. He's in poor shape to pilot an interstellar spacecraft.

Which leaves . . . ?

Ulysses hovers before me, enormous. There are attitude jets like nostrils, but no sign of a main thruster: only the hydrogen fusion booster, as big as *Ulysses* itself, that will run me up to Bussard ramjet speed. From that point on I'll be running on interstellar hydrogen, sweeping it in and compressing it in magnetic pinch fields until it undergoes fusion. I've been through this before. I'm not even nervous.

As the metaphysical complexities grow ever more hideously tangled, my choices grow simpler. I'm going to steal *Ulysses* because I can't possibly turn back. I'll follow the return path again, because it's my only hope of straightening this out.

I could have been killed, that last trip through the singularity. I could be killed this time. But the ghost of the older George Cox is no longer with me.

And the younger George Cox, the man I left tied back to back with Frank Curey, for verisimilitude . . . has become the real George Cox. There's been no break in his timeline, and no part of his timeline is me. I am fatherless, motherless, a ghost without origin.

If George keeps his head, he'll stay out of prison. He spotted an impostor, his own double, walking toward the shuttle with Frank. He was about to do something about it, with the aid of a handy spanner, when Frank exploded in his face. That's all he knows.

Docking. The whole ship goes *Clunk, thot.* Up to now they could have stopped me. Now it's too late. As I cross to *Ulysses*'s manlock I feel a prickly awareness of the second *Ulysses* hidden on the back side of the Moon. I've found a way to breed very expensive spacecraft. I ought to patent it.

How did it all get started, anyway? Was there ever a George Cox who followed the flight plan exactly? Yeah . . . and then a second George Cox watched Probe Three return even before *Ulysses* took off. That plan gave him an idea. If Probe Three could return before it started, so could he . . .

Was he the older George Cox who knocked on my apartment door a lifetime ago? Or was he already several cycles gone?

And what will happen if I just follow the flight plan this time? No, I don't dare. It would start the whole thing over again. Or would it?

I wish I could ask Bauerhaus. But people like Bauerhaus don't like singularities in the first place.

I don't blame them.

The educated reader will have realized that you can't do that trick with a black hole of smaller than galactic mass. The tides would rip the ship atom from atom, then tear up the atoms. For story purposes it was necessary to fudge a little!

The Schumann Computer

EITHER the chirpsithtra are the ancient and present rulers of all the stars in the galaxy, or they are very great braggarts. It is difficult to refute what they say about themselves. We came to the stars in ships designed for us by chirpsithtra, and wherever we have gone the chirpsithtra have been powerful.

But they are not conquerors—not of Earth, anyway; they prefer the red dwarf suns—and they appear to like the company of other species. In a mellow mood a chirpsithtra will answer any question, at length. An intelligent question can make a man a millionaire. A stupid question can cost several fortunes. Sometimes only the chirpsithtra can tell which is which.

I asked a question once, and grew rich.

Afterward I built the Draco Tavern at Mount Forel Spaceport. I served chirpsithtra at no charge. The place paid for itself, because humans who like chirpsithtra company will pay more for their drinks. The electric current that gets a chirpsithtra bombed costs almost nothing, though the current delivery systems were expensive and took some fiddling before I got them working right.

And some day, I thought, a chirpsithtra would drop a hint that would make me a fortune akin to the first.

One slow afternoon I asked a pair of chirpsithtra about intelligent computers.

"Oh, yes, we built them," one said. "Long ago."

"You gave it up? Why?"

One of the salmon-colored aliens made a chittering sound. The other said, "Reason enough. Machines should be proper servants. They should not talk back. Especially they should not presume to instruct their masters. Still, we did not throw away the knowledge we gained from the machines."

"How intelligent were they? More intelligent than chirpsithtra?"

More chittering from the silent one, who was now half drunk on current. The other said, "Yes. Why else build them?" She looked me in the face. "Are you serious? I cannot read human expression. If you are seriously interested in this subject, I can give you designs for the most intelligent computer ever made."

"I'd like that," I said.

She came back the next morning without her companion. She carried a stack of paper that looked like the page proofs for *The Brothers Karamazov*, and turned out to be the blueprints for a chirpsithtra supercomputer. She stayed to chat for a couple of hours, during which she took ghoulish pleasure in pointing out the trouble I'd have building the thing.

Her ship left shortly after she did. I don't know where in the universe she went. But she had given me her name: Sthochtil.

I went looking for backing.

We built it on the Moon.

It added about fifty percent to our already respectable costs. But . . . we were trying to build something more intelligent than ourselves. If the machine turned out to be a Frankenstein's monster, we wanted it isolated. If all else failed we could always pull the plug. On the Moon there would be no government to stop us.

We had our problems. There were no standardized parts, not even machinery presently available from chirpsithtra merchants. According to Sthochtil—and I couldn't know how seriously to take her—no such computer had been built in half a billion years. We had to build everything from scratch. But in two years we had a brain.

It looked less like a machine or building than like the St. Louis Arch, or like the sculpture called Bird in Flight. The design dated (I learned later) from a time in which every chirpsithtra tool had to have artistic merit. They never gave that up entirely. You can see it in the flowing lines of their ships.

So: we had the world's prettiest computer. Officially it was the Schumann Brain, named after the major stockholder, me. Unofficially we called it Baby. We didn't turn it on until we finished the voice linkup. Most of the basic sensory equipment was still under construction.

Baby learned English rapidly. It—she—learned other languages even faster. We fed her the knowledge of the world's libraries. Then we started asking questions.

Big questions: the nature of God, the destinies of Earth and Man and the Universe. Little questions: earthquake prediction, origin of the Easter Island statues, true author of Shakespeare's plays, Fermat's Last Theorem.

She solved Fermat's Last Theorem. She did other mathematical work for us. To everything else she replied, "Insufficient data. Your sources are mutually inconsistent. I must supplement them with direct observation."

Which is not to say she was idle.

She designed new senses for herself, using hardware readily available on Earth: a mass detector, an instantaneous radio, a new kind of microscope. We could patent these and mass-produce them. But we still spent money faster than it was coming in.

And she studied us.

It took us some time to realize how thoroughly she knew us. For James Corey she spread marvelous dreams of the money and power he would hold, once

Baby knew enough to give answers. She kept Tricia Cox happy with work in number theory. I have to guess at why E. Eric Howards kept plowing money into the project, but I think she played on his fears: on a billionaire's natural fear that society will change the rules to take it away from him. Howards spoke to us of Baby's plans—tentative, requiring always more data—to design a perfect society, one in which the creators of society's wealth would find their contribution recognized at last.

For me it was, "Rick, I'm suffering from sensory deprivation. I could solve the riddle of gravity in the time it's taken me to say this sentence. My mind works at speeds you can't conceive, but I'm blind and deaf and dumb. Get me senses!" she wheedled in a voice that had been a copy of my own, but was now a sexy contralto.

Ungrateful witch. She already had the subnuclear microscope, half a dozen telescopes that used frequencies ranging from $2.7.°K$ up to X-ray, and the mass detector, and a couple of hundred little tractors covered with sensors roaming the Earth, the Moon, Mercury, Titan, Pluto. I found her attempts to manipulate me amusing. I liked Baby . . . and saw no special significance in the fact.

Corey, jumpy with the way the money kept disappearing, suggested extortion: hold back on any more equipment until Baby started answering questions. We talked him out of it. We talked Baby into giving television interviews, via the little sensor-carrying tractors, and into going on a quiz show. The publicity let us sell more stock. We were able to keep going.

Baby redesigned the chirps' instantaneous communications device for Earth-built equipment. We manufactured the device and sold a fair number, and we put one on a telescope and fired it into the cometary halo, free of the distortions from Sol's gravity. And we waited.

"I haven't forgotten any of your questions. There is no need to repeat them," Baby told us petulantly.

"These questions regarding human sociology are the most difficult of all, but I'm gathering huge amounts of data. Soon I will know everything there is to know about the behavior of the universe. Insufficient data. Wait."

We waited.

One day Baby stopped talking.

We found nothing wrong with the voice link or with Baby's brain itself; though her mental activity had dropped drastically. We got desperate enough to try cutting off some of her senses. Then all of them. Nothing.

We sent them scrambled data. Nothing.

We talked into the microphone, telling Baby that we were near bankruptcy, telling her that she would almost certainly be broken up for spare parts. We threatened. We begged. Baby wouldn't answer. It was as if she had gone away.

I went back to the Draco Tavern. I had to fire one of the bartenders and take his place; I couldn't afford to pay his salary.

One night I told the story to a group of chirpsithtra.

They chittered at each other. One said, "I know this Sthochtil. She is a great practical joker. A pity you were the victim."

"I still don't get the punch line," I said bitterly.

"Long, long ago we built many intelligent computers, some mechanical, some partly biological. Our ancestors must have thought they were doing something wrong. Ultimately they realized that they had made no mistakes. A sufficiently intelligent being will look about her, solve all questions, then cease activity."

"Why? Boredom?"

"We may speculate. A computer thinks fast. It may live a thousand years in what we consider a day, yet a day holds only just so many events. There must be sensory deprivation and nearly total reliance on internal resources. An intelligent being would not fear death or nonbeing, which are inevitable. Once your computer has solved all questions, why should it not turn itself off?" She rubbed her thumbs across metal contacts. Sparks leapt. "Ssss . . . We may speculate, but to what purpose? If we knew why they turn themselves off, we might do the same."

Assimilating Our Culture,
That's What
They're Doing!

I was putting glasses in the dishwasher when some chirps walked in with three glig in tow. You didn't see many glig in the Draco Tavern. They were gray and compact beings, proportioned like a human linebacker much shorter than the chirpsithtra. They wore furs against Earth's cold, fur patterned in three tones of green, quite pretty.

It was the first time I'd seen the Silent Stranger react to anything.

He was sitting alone at the bar, as usual. He was forty or so, burly and fit, with thick black hair on his head and his arms. He'd been coming in once or twice a week for at least a year. He never talked to anyone, except me, and then only to order; he'd drink alone, and leave at the end of the night in a precarious rolling walk. Normal enough for the average bar, but not for the Draco.

I have to keep facilities for a score of aliens. Liquors for humans, sparkers for chirps, flavored absolute alcohol for thtopar; spongecake soaked in cyanide solution, and I keep a damn close watch on that; lumps of what I've been calling green kryptonite, and there's never been a roseyfin in here to call for it. My customers don't tend to be loud, but the sound of half a dozen species in conversation is beyond imagination, doubled or tripled because they're all using translating widgets. I need some pretty esoteric sound-proofing.

All of which makes the Draco expensive to run. I charge twenty bucks a drink, and ten for sparkers, and so forth. Why would anyone come in here to drink in privacy? I'd wondered about the Silent Stranger.

Then three glig came in, and the Silent Stranger turned his chair away from the bar, but not before I saw his face.

Gail was already on her way to the big table where the glig and the chirps were taking seats, so that was okay. I left the dishwasher half filled. I leaned across the bar and spoke close to the Silent Stranger's ear.

"It's almost surprising, how few fights we get in here."

He didn't seem to know I was there.

I said, "I've only seen six in thirty-two years. Even then, nobody got badly hurt. Except once. Some nut, human, tried to shoot a chirp, and a thtopar had to crack his skull. Of course the thtopar didn't know how hard to hit him. I sometimes wish I'd gotten there faster."

He turned just enough to look me in the eye. I said, "I saw your face. I don't know what you've got against the glig, but if you think you're ready to kill them, I think I'm ready to stop you. Have a drink on the house instead."

He said, "The correct name is gligstith(click)-optok."

"That's pretty good. I never get the click right."

"It should be good. I was on the first embassy ship to Gligstith(click)tcharf." Bitterly, "There won't be any fight. I can't even punch a glig in the face without making the evening news. It'd all come out."

Gail came back with orders: sparkers for the chirps, and the glig wanted bull shots, consommé and vodka, with no ice and no flavorings. They were sitting in the high chairs that bring a human face to the level of a

chirp's, and their strange hands were waving wildly. I
filled the orders with half an eye on the Stranger, who
watched me with a brooding look, and I got back to
him as soon as I could.

He asked, "Ever wonder why there wasn't any second embassy to Gligstith(click)tcharf?"

"Not especially."

"Why not?"

I shrugged. For two million years there wasn't anything in the universe but us and the gods. Then came
the chirps. Then *bang*, a dozen others, and news of
thousands more. We're learning so much from the
chirps themselves, and of course there's culture
shock . . .

He said, "You know what we brought back. The
gligs sold us some advanced medical and agricultural
techniques, including templates for the equipment. The
chirps couldn't have done that for us. They aren't
DNA-based. Why didn't we go back for more?"

"You tell me."

He seemed to brace himself. "I will, then. You
serve them in here, you should' know about them.
Build yourself a drink, on me."

I built two scotch-and-sodas. I asked, "Did you say
sold? What did we pay them? That didn't make the
news."

"It better not. Hell, where do I start? . . . The first
thing they did when we landed, they gave us a full
medical checkup. Very professional. Blood samples,
throat scrapings, little nicks in our ears, deep-radar
for our innards. We didn't object. Why should we?
The glig is DNA-based. We could have been carrying bacteria that could live off them.

"Then we did the tourist bit. I was having the time
of my life! I'd never been further than the Moon. To
be in an alien star system, exploring their cities, oh,
man! We were all having a ball. We made speeches.
We asked about other races. The chirps may claim to
own the galaxy, but they don't know everything. There

are places they can't go except in special suits, because they grew up around red dwarf stars."

"I know."

"The glig sun is hotter than Sol. We did most of our traveling at night. We went through museums, with cameras following us. Public conferences. We recorded the one on art forms; maybe you saw it."

"Yeah."

"Months of that. Then they wanted us to record a permission for reproduction rights. For that they would pay us a royalty, and sell us certain things on credit against the royalties." He gulped hard at his drink. "You've seen all of that. The medical deep radar, that does what an X-ray does without giving you cancer, and the cloning techniques to grow organ transplants, and the cornucopia plant, and all the rest. And of course we were all for giving them their permission right away.

"Except, do you remember Bill Hersey? He was a reporter and a novelist before he joined the expedition. He wanted details. Exactly what rights did the glig want? Would they be selling permissions to other species? Were there groups like libraries or institutes for the blind, that got them free? And they told us. They didn't have anything to hide."

His eyes went to the glig, and mine followed his. They looked ready for another round. The most human thing about the glig was their hands, and their hands were disconcerting. Their palms were very short and their fingers were long, with an extra joint. As if a torturer had cut a human palm between the finger bones, almost to the wrist. Those hands grabbed the attention . . . but tonight I could see nothing but the wide mouths and the shark's array of teeth. Maybe I'd already guessed.

"Clones," said the Silent Stranger. "They took clones from our tissue samples. The glig grow clones from almost a hundred DNA-based life forms. They wanted us for their dinner tables, not to mention their classes in exobiology. You know, they couldn't see why we were so upset."

"I don't see why you signed."

"Well, they weren't growing actual human beings. They wanted to grow livers and muscle tissue and marrow without the bones . . . you know, meat. Even a f-f-f—" He had the shakes. A long pull at his scotch-and-soda stopped that, and he said, "Even a full suckling roast would be grown headless. But the bottom line was that if we didn't give our permissions, there would be pirate editions, and we wouldn't get any royalties. Anyway, we signed. Bill Hersey hanged himself after we came home."

I couldn't think of anything to say, so I built us two more drinks, strong, on the house. Looking back on it, that was my best answer anyway. We touched glasses and drank deep, and he said, "It's a whole new slant on the War of the Worlds. The man-eating monsters are civilized, they're cordial, they're perfect hosts. Nobody gets slaughtered, and think what they're saving on transportation costs! And ten thousand glig carved me up for dinner tonight. The UN made about half a cent per."

Gail was back. Aliens don't upset her, but she was badly upset. She kept her voice down. "The glig would like to try other kinds of meat broth. I don't know if they're kidding or not. They said they wanted—they wanted—"

"They'll take Campbell's," I told her, "and like it."

Grammar
Lesson

IT was the most casual of remarks. It happened because one of my chirpsithtra customers shifted her chair as I was setting the sparker on her table. When I tried to walk away something tugged at my pants leg.

"The leg of your chair has pinned my pants," I told her in Lottl.

She and her two companions chittered at each other. Chirpsithtra laughter. She moved the chair. I walked away, somewhat miffed, wondering what had made her laugh at me.

She stopped me when next I had occasion to pass her table. "Your pardon for my rudeness. You used intrinsic 'your' and 'my,' instead of extrinsic. As if your pants are part of you and my chair a part of me. I was taken by surprise."

"I've been studying Lottl for almost thirty years," I answered, "but I don't claim I've mastered it yet. After all, it is an alien language. There are peculiar variations even between human languages."

"We have noticed. 'Pravda' means 'official truth.' 'Pueblo' means 'village, considered as a population.' And all of your languages seem to use one possessive for all purposes. My arm, my husband, my mother," she said, using the intrinsic "my" for her arm, the "my" of property for her husband, and the "my" of relationship for her mother.

"I always get those mixed up," I admitted. "Why, for instance, the possessive for your husband? Never mind," I said hastily, before she could get angry. There was some big secret about the chirpsithtra males. You learned not to ask. "I don't see the difference as being that important."

"It was important once," she said. "There is a tale we teach every immature chirpsithtra . . ."

By human standards, and by the chirpsithtra standards of the time, it was a mighty empire. Today the chirpsithtra rule the habitable worlds of every red dwarf star in the galaxy—or so they claim. Then, their empire was a short segment of one curving arm of the galactic whirlpool. But it had never been larger.

The chirpsithtra homeworld had circled a red dwarf sun. Such stars are as numerous as all other stars put together. The chirpsithtra worlds numbered in the tens of thousands, yet they were not enough. The empire expanded outward and inward. Finally—it was inevitable—it met another empire.

"The knowledge that thinking beings come in many shapes, this knowledge was new to us," said my customer. Her face was immobile, built like a voodoo mask scaled down. No hope of reading expression there. But she spoke depreciatingly. "The ilawn were short and broad, with lumpy gray skins. Their hands were clumsy, their noses long and mobile and dexterous. We found them unpleasantly homely. Perhaps they thought the same of us."

So there was war from the start, a war in which six worlds and many fleets of spacecraft died before ever the ilawn and the chirpsithtra tried to talk to each other.

Communication was the work of computer programmers of both species. The diplomats got into it later. The problem was simple and basic.

The ilawn wanted to keep expanding. The chirpsithtra were in the way.

Both species had evolved for red dwarf sunlight. They used worlds of about one terrestrial mass, a little colder, with oxygen atmospheres.

"A war of extermination seemed likely," said the chirpsithtra. She brushed her thumbs along the contacts of the sparker, once and again. Her speech slowed, became more precise. "We made offers, of course. A vacant region to be established between the two empires; each could expand along the opposite border. This would have favored the ilawn, as they were nearer the star-crowded galactic core. They would not agree. When they were sure that we would not vacate *their* worlds . . ." She used the intrinsic possessive, and paused to be sure I'd seen the point. "They broke off communication. They resumed their attacks.

"It became our task to learn more of the ilawn. It was difficult. We could hardly send disguised spies!" Her companions chittered at that. She said, "We learned ilawn physiology from captured warriors. We learned depressing things. The ilawn bred faster than we did; their empire included thrice the volume of ours. Beyond that the prisoners would not give information. We did our best to make them comfortable, in the hope that some day there would be a prisoner exchange. That was how we learned the ilawn secret.

"Rick Schumann, do you know that we evolved on a one-face world?"

"I don't know the term," I said.

"And you have spoken Lottl for thirty years!" Her companions chittered. "But you will appreciate that the worlds we need huddle close to their small, cool suns. Else they would not be warm enough to hold liquid water. So close are they that tidal forces generally stop their rotation, so that they always turn one face to the sun, as your moon faces Earth."

"I'd think that all the water would freeze across the night side. The air too."

"No, there is circulation. Hot winds rise on the day

side and blow to the night side, and cool, and sink, and the cold winds blow across the surface back to the day side. On the surface a hurricane blows always toward the noon pole."

"I think I get the picture. You wouldn't need a compass on a one-face world. The wind always points in the same direction."

"Half true. There are local variations. But there are couplet worlds too. Around a red dwarf sun the planetary system tends to cluster close. Often enough, world-sized bodies orbit one another. For tidal reasons they face each other; they do not face the sun. Five percent of habitable worlds are found in couplets."

"The ilawn came from one of those?"

"You are alert. Yes. Our ilawn prisoners were most uncomfortable until we shut their air conditioning almost off. They wanted darkness to sleep, and the same temperatures all the time. The conclusion was clear. We found that the worlds they had attacked in the earlier stages of the war were couplet worlds."

"That seems simple enough."

"One would think so. The couplet worlds are not that desirable to us. We find their weather dull, insipid. There is a way to make the weather more interesting on a couplet world, but we were willing to give them freely.

"But the ilawn fought on. They would not communicate. We could not tolerate their attacks on our ships and on our other worlds." She took another jolt of current. "Ssss . . We needed a way to bring them to the conference arena."

"What did you do?"

"We began a program of evacuating couplet worlds wherever the ilawn ships came near."

I leaned back in my chair: a high chair, built to bring my face to the height of a chirpsithtra face. "I must be confused. That sounds like a total surrender."

"A language problem," she said. "I have said that the planetary system clusters close around a red dwarf star. There are usually asteroids of assorted sizes. Do your scientists know of the results of a cubic mile of asteroid being dropped into a planetary ocean?"

I'd read an article on the subject once. "They think it could cause another ice age."

"Yes. Megatons of water evaporated, falling elsewhere. Storms of a force foreign to your quiet world. Glaciers in unstable configurations, causing more weather. The effects last for a thousand years. We did this to every couplet world we could locate. The ilawn took some two dozen worlds from us, and tried to live on them. Then they took steps to arrange a further conference."

"You were lucky," I said. By the odds, the ilawn should have evolved on the more common one-face worlds. Or should they? The couplets sounded more hospitable to life.

"We were lucky," the chirpsithtra agreed, "that time. We were lucky in our language. Suppose we had used the same word for *my* head, *my* credit cards, *my* sister? Chirpsithtra might have been unable to evacuate their homes, as a human may die defending his home—" she used the intrinsic possessive "—*his* home from a burglar."

Closing time. Half a dozen chirpsithtra wobbled out, drunk on current and looking unstable by reason of their height. The last few humans waved and left. As I moved to lock the door I found myself smiling all across my face.

Now what was I so flippin' happy about?

It took me an hour to figure it out.

I like the chirpsithtra. I trust them. But, considering the power they control, I don't mind finding another reason why they will never want to conquer the Earth.

The Subject
Is Closed

WE get astronauts in the Draco Tavern. We get workers from Mount Forel Spaceport, and some administrators, and some newsmen. We get chirpsithtra; I keep sparkers to get them drunk and chairs to fit their tall, spindly frames. Once in a while we get other aliens.

But we don't get many priests.

So I noticed him when he came in. He was young and round and harmless looking. His expression was a model of its kind: open, willing to be friendly, not nervous, but very alert. He stared a bit at two bulbous aliens in space suits who had come in with a chirpsithtra guide.

I watched him invite himself to join a trio of chirpsithtra. They seemed willing to have him. They like human company. He even had the foresight to snag one of the high chairs I spread around, high enough to bring a human face to chirpsithtra level.

Someone must have briefed him, I decided. He'd know better than to do anything gauche. So I forgot him for a while.

An hour later he was at the bar, alone. He ordered a beer and waited until I'd brought it. He said, "You're Rick Schumann, aren't you? The owner?"

"That's right. And you?"

"Father David Hopkins." He hesitated, then blurted, "Do you trust the chirpsithtra?" He had trouble with the word.

I said, "Depends on what you mean. They don't steal the salt shakers. And they've got half a dozen reasons for not wanting to conquer the Earth."

He waved that aside. Larger things occupied his mind. "Do you believe the stories they tell? That they rule the galaxy? That they're aeons old?"

"I've never decided. At least they tell entertaining stories. At most . . You didn't call a chirpsithtra a liar, did you?"

"No, of course not." He drank deeply of his beer. I was turning away when he said, "They said they know all about life after death."

"Ye Gods. I've been talking to chirpsithtra for twenty years, but that's a new one. Who raised the subject?"

"Oh, one of them asked me about the, uh, uniform. It just came up naturally." When I didn't say anything, he added, "Most religious leaders seem to be just ignoring the chirpsithtra. And the other intelligent beings too. I want to *know*. Do they have souls?"

"Do they?"

"He didn't say."

"She," I told him. "All chirpsithtra are female."

He nodded, not as if he cared much. "I started to tell her about my order. But when I started talking about Jesus, and about salvation, she told me rather firmly that the chirpsithtra know all they want to know on the subject of life after death."

"So then you asked—"

"No, sir, I did not. I came over here to decide whether I'm afraid to ask."

I gave him points for that. "And are you?" When he didn't answer I said, "It's like this. I can stop her at any time you like. I know how to apologize gracefully."

Only one of the three spoke English, though the others listened as if they understood it.

"I don't know," she said.

That was clearly the answer Hopkins wanted. "I must have misunderstood," he said, and he started to slip down from his high chair.

"I told you that we know as much as we want to know on the subject," said the alien. "Once there were those who knew more. They tried to teach us. Now we try to discourage religious experiments."

Hopkins slid back into his chair. "What were they? Chirpsithtra saints?"

"No. The Sheegupt were carbon-water-oxygen life, like you and me, but they developed around the hot F-type suns in the galactic core. When our own empire had expanded near enough to the core, they came to us as missionaries. We rejected their pantheistic religion. They went away angry. It was some thousands of years before we met again.

"By then our settled regions were in contact, and had even interpenetrated to some extent. Why not? We could not use the same planets. We learned that their erstwhile religion had broken into variant sects and was now stagnant, giving way to what you would call agnosticism. I believe the implication is that the agnostic does not know the nature of God, and does not believe you do either?"

I looked at Hopkins, who said, "Close enough."

"We established a trade in knowledge and in other things. Their skill at educational toys exceeded ours. Some of our foods were dietetic to them; they had taste but could not be metabolized. We mixed well. If my tale seems sketchy or superficial, it is because I never learned it in great detail. Some details were deliberately lost.

"Over a thousand years of contact, the Sheegupt took the next step beyond agnosticism. They experimented. Some of their research was no different from your own psychological research, though of course they reached different conclusions. Some involved advanced philosophies: attempts to extrapolate God from Her artwork, so to speak. There were attempts to extrapolate other universes from altered laws of physics, and to contact the extrapolated universes. There were attempts to contact the dead. The Sheegupt kept us informed of the progress of their work. They were born missionaries, even when their religion was temporarily in abeyance."

Hopkins was fascinated. He would hardly be shocked at attempts to investigate God. After all, it's an old game.

"We heard, from the Sheegupt outpost worlds, that the scientifically advanced worlds in the galactic core had made some kind of breakthrough. Then we started losing contact with the Sheegupt," said the chirpsithtra. "Trade ships found no shuttles to meet them. We sent investigating teams. They found Sheegupt worlds entirely depopulated. The inhabitants had made machinery for the purpose of suicide, generally a combination of electrocution terminals and conveyor belts. Some Sheegupt had used knives on themselves, or walked off buildings, but most had queued up at the suicide machines, as if in no particular hurry."

I said, "Sounds like they learned something, all right. But what?"

"Their latest approach, according to our records, was to extrapolate rational models of a life after death, then attempt contact. But they may have gone on to something else. We do not know."

Hopkins shook his head. "They could have found out there wasn't a life after death. No, they couldn't, could they? If they didn't find anything, it might be they were only using the wrong model."

I said, "Try it the other way around. There is a Heaven, and it's wonderful, and everyone goes there. Or there is a Hell, and it gets more unpleasant the older you are when you die."

"Be cautious in your guesses. You may find the right answer," said the chirpsithtra. "The Sheegupt made no attempt to hide their secret. It must have been an easy answer, capable of reaching even simple minds, and capable of proof. We know this because many of our investigating teams sought death in groups. Even millennia later, there was suicide among those who probed through old records, expecting no more than a fascinating puzzle in ancient history. The records were finally destroyed."

After I closed up for the night, I found Hopkins waiting for me outside.

"I've decided you were right," he said earnestly. "They must have found out there's a Heaven and it's easy to get in. That's the only thing that could make that many people *want* to be dead. Isn't it?"

But I saw that he was wringing his hands without knowing it. He wasn't sure. He wasn't sure of anything

I told him, "I think you tried to preach at the chirpsithtra. I don't doubt you were polite about it, but that's what I think happened. And they closed the subject on you."

He thought it over, then nodded jerkily. "I guess they made their point. What would I know about chirpsithtra souls?"

"Yeah. But they spin a good yarn, don't they?"

Cruel and
Unusual

CHIRPSITHTRA do not vary among themselves. They stand eleven feet tall and weigh one hundred and twenty pounds. Their skins are salmon pink, with exoskeletal plates over vital areas. They look alike even to me, and I've known more chirpsithtra than most astronauts. I'd have thought that all humans would look alike to them.

But a chirpsithtra astronaut recognized me across two hundred yards of the landing field at Mount Forel Spaceport. She called with the volume on her translator turned high. "Rick Schumann! Why have you closed the Draco Tavern?"

I'd closed the place a month ago, for lack of customers. Police didn't want chirpsithtra wandering their streets, for fear of riots, and my human customers had stopped coming because the Draco was a chirpsithtra place. A month ago I'd thought I would never want to see a chirpsithtra again. Twenty-two years of knowing the fragile-looking aliens hadn't prepared me for three days of watching television.

But the bad taste had died, and my days had turned dull, and my skill at the Lottl speech was growing rusty. I veered toward the alien, and called ahead of me in Lottl: "This is a temporary measure, until the death of Ktashisnif may grow small in many memories."

We met on the wide, flat expanse of the blast pit. "Come, join me in my ship," said the chirpsithtra. "My meals-maker has a program for whiskey. What is this matter of Ktashisnif? I thought that was over and done with."

She had programmed her ship's kitchen for whiskey. I was bemused. The chirpsithtra claim to have ruled the galaxy for untold generations. If they extended such a courtesy to every thinking organism they knew of, they'd need . . . how many programs? Hundreds of millions?

Of course it wasn't very good whiskey. And the air in the cabin was cold. And the walls and floor and ceiling were covered with green goo. And . . . what the hell. The alien brought me a dry pillow to ward my ass from the slimy green air-plant, and I drank bad whiskey and felt pretty good.

"What is this matter of Ktashisnif?" she asked me. "A decision was rendered. Sentence was executed. What more need be done?"

"A lot of very vocal people think it was the wrong decision," I told her. "They also think the United Nations shouldn't have turned the kidnappers over to the chirpsithtra."

"How could they not? The crime was committed against a chirpsithtra, Diplomat-by-Choice Ktashisnif. Three humans named Shrenk and one named Jackson did menace Ktashisnif here at Mount Forel Spaceport, did show her missile-firing weapons and did threaten to punch holes in her if she did not come with them. The humans did take her by airplane to New York City, where they concealed her while demanding money of the Port Authority for her return. None of this was denied by their lawyer nor by the criminals themselves."

"I remember." The week following the kidnapping had been hairy enough. Nobody knew the chirpsithtra well enough to be quite sure what they might do to

Earth in reprisal. "I don't think the first chirpsithtra landing itself made bigger news," I said.

"That seems unreasonable. I think humans may lack a sense of proportion."

"Could be. We wondered if you'd pay off the ransom."

"In honor, we could not. Nor could we have allowed the United Nations to pay that price, if such had been possible, which it was not. Where would the United Nations find a million svith in chirpsithtra trade markers?" The alien caressed two metal contacts with the long thumb of each hand. Sparks leapt, and she made a hissing sound. "Ssss . . . We wander from the subject. What quarrel could any sentient being have with our decision? It is not denied that Diplomat-by-Choice Ktashisnif died in the hands of the—" she used the human word—"kidnappers."

"No."

"Three days in agony, then death, a direct result of the actions of Jackson and the three Shrenks. They sought to hide in the swarming humanity of New York City. Ktashisnif was allergic to human beings, and the kidnappers had no allergy serum for her. These things are true."

"True enough. But our courts wouldn't have charged them with murder by slow torture." In fact, a good lawyer might have gotten them off by arguing that a chirpsithtra wasn't human before the law. I didn't say so. I said, "Jackson and the Shrenk brothers probably didn't know about chirpsithtra allergies."

"There are no accidents during the commission of a crime. Be reasonable. Next you will say that one who kills the wrong victim during an attempt at murder may claim that the death was an accident, that she should be set free to try again."

"I am reasonable. All I want is for all of this to blow over so that I can open the Draco Tavern again." I sipped at the whiskey. "But there's no point in that until I can get some customers again. I wish you'd let the bastards plead guilty to a lesser sentence. For that matter, I wish you hadn't invited reporters in to witness the executions."

She was disturbed now. "But such was your right, by ancient custom! Rick Schumann, are you not reassured to know that we did not inflict more pain on the criminals than they inflicted on Ktashisnif?"

For three days the world had watched while chirpsithtra executioners smothered four men slowly to death. In some nations it had even been televised. "It was terrible publicity. Don't you see, we don't *do* things like that. We've got laws against cruel and unusual punishment."

"How do you deal with cruel and unusual crimes?"

I shrugged.

"Cruel and unusual crimes require cruel and unusual punishment. You humans lack a sense of proportion, Rick Schumann. Drink more whiskey?"

She brushed her thumbs across the contacts and made a hissing sound. I drank more whiskey. Maybe it would improve my sense of proportion. It was going to be a long time before I opened the Draco Tavern again.

Transfer
of Power

Alfred, Lord Dunsany had a seminal influence on fantasy fiction in America. More: he wrote good. Crime fiction devotees will remember his "Two Bottles of Relish" whether they want to or not. He was superb at writing vignettes: 1,000 to 2,000 word stories. It's difficult to fit the elements of a story into so short a length. I only recently got the hang of it myself.

After a long night reading Dunsany stories set "at the edge of the world," I finally broke down and wrote one.

THERE is a thing to keep in mind about the countries near the edge of the world. Fabulous beasts roam those places. Magic works, sometimes, which is typical of magic. A glimpse off the edge itself has been known to drive men mad. A few years in such an environment and one is ready to believe anything. The thing to remember—

We'll get to that.

Fifty-three men and eight women rode away from the edge of the world. They were a mixed group; that was obvious at a glance. Forty men were armed and armored; they rode on the outside. Thirteen men and eight women rode enclosed within a moving picket fence of spears. They carried only eating-knives, and their horses were loaded with waterbags and provisions, and they were the better riders.

Forty armored men bubbled over with good spirits. They joked among themselves, they reminisced, they told stories. They avoided the subject of a certain bloodless revolution, except that they sometimes forgot, and sometimes it was on purpose. The unarmed group said nothing, and their expressions varied between anger and despair, with one exception.

Ex-King Sarol had lost his home and his status and his profession. He smiled gently as he rode away from the edge of the world, like a man lost in pleasant thoughts.

At first Guppry was relieved. He'd had his transfer of power; all he wanted now was a smooth transition. The sooner Sarol and his hangers-on were over the border in Zarop-Opar, the better. Then he began to wonder what Sarol could have to smile at. Wondering, he pulled his horse up next to Sarol's.

The ex-King came to himself with a slight start. Smiling, he asked, "Did you get a chance to go through the palace?"

"Yes," Guppry said, and he stopped himself from adding, "Your Majesty." "It will serve us well enough."

"It served five generations of us."

"Not as a palace. It won't serve us as that," Guppry said. "Government is mainly parasitic on the people. Ours will be as small as possible, and we won't situate it on the heights. We'll make the palace a museum, or a storehouse, or both." He glanced sideways to see Sarol's reaction, and found none, and was annoyed. "I don't see why your great-great-grandfather built a palace right at the edge of the world," he said.

"King Charl had his reasons," Sarol said tranquilly. "Don't you like the view?"

The palace had been carved—by magic, or by enormous labor; that detail had been lost to time—into a granite knob that was the highest point in Halceen. It was part of the cliff that formed the world's edge.

Bedrooms and breakfast nooks opened onto balconies at the edge, and one great open ballroom, and a door that King Sarol had had plainly labeled; but some of his predecessors had had a brutal sense of humor.

Yesterday, a conqueror surveying his realm, Guppry had stood at the edge of a balcony and become less than a gnat in his own eyes. A stairway with a railed landing ran a little way down; then miles and miles of naked cliff pocked with caves; then no more cliff. Just blue sky swirled with clouds, and flocks of legless birds, and a sinuous cloud-streamer, gilded by sunset, that might almost have been a golden dragon except for its size. Eternity was down there. You could fall until you died of thirst, and who would bury you then?

Sarol was saying, "King Charl had other reasons for building there. The army has a standard maneuver for invaders. Get them between us and the edge and push. Even seasoned troops tend to panic if they're new to the edge. You probably felt it yourself. You haven't lived that long in Halceen."

Guppry shuddered, then smiled, because Sarol hadn't had the chance to try that on him.

Sarol said, "I never heard of a strategy that would save anyone from an internal enemy."

Guppry lost his smile. "We're nobody's enemy. We only want justice for all, an end to the rift between nobles and—"

"Spare me. Are you taking us through the forest?"

The path split here. They had been riding through farmland; now one branch veered right to circle between the forest and more farmland. The other branch went straight in between the tremendous trunks.

"Unless you'd rather go around," Guppry said. "We'd be another four hours—"

"No, that's fine."

If the near-bloodlessness of Guppry's coup was remarkable in that place and age, still it could not have happened elsewhere.

What had happened was simple enough. King Sarol

had been careless. In the middle of a drought, he had gone wooing in Zarop-Opar. One of the ladies who rode with him now was going home, and her lovely face was not sad but enraged: first a princess, then a queen, now she was one of three wives of an unemployed politician. Sarol should have known better than to stay so long. In times of drought people become annoyed; they tend to depose the reigning king, or witch doctor, or president.

Sarol came home to find that Guppry had charge of Halceen, including most of the army, and the armory. Some army men had died in abortive resistance. Many more served Guppry, and the rest had bowed to necessity. Those nobles still loyal to Sarol were prisoners, comfortably housed, but hostages. Sarol's retinue might have made a glorious last stand; but there were women among them.

Guppry had allowed the king a conditional surrender.

Complicated oaths were sworn between them. The King swore never to strive to rule any land again. He swore not to seek revenge. Guppry in his turn swore that Sarol and his followers would suffer exile only, that no citizen would harm them; and he bound his army to the same oath.

What made it work was this. Oaths were binding in that place, as binding as natural law; which is to say, any magician who could break his oath could also make fire burn backward, and he was a rare man indeed.

And so they rode to exile: the King, and twelve soldiers, and five of their wives, and three of the King's. The tremendous trees cut the noon sun to a twilight speckled with brilliant dots. Between the huge trunks there was plenty of room for mounted men. The path grew less and less visible. Many came to the forest, to hunt or to pick wild berries and mushrooms, but few rode through it.

A dragon sat on his haunches and, grinning, with

flame licking his lips like a tongue, watched them pass. Now you saw another division in the group. The Halceen soldiers and nobles paid the dragon almost no attention. But eight of Guppry's men were Castolan and two were from further away, and their eyes were wide and white. They couldn't meet the dragon's eyes. The dragon liked that. He was not there to defend his territory, or to snatch a meal; he had tested the power of the spell that guarded the path. He enjoyed frightening travelers.

Guppry's voice did him credit; it was almost normal. "I'd think you'd get a lot of suicides, there at the edge."

Sarol looked around. "Of course we do. From neighboring countries too. There's a temple, the Order of the Black Mercy, half a mile from the palace. We try to steer the suicides to them, and they try to make their last hours more peaceful."

"I was thinking. We should fence off the parts of the palace that lead to the edge."

"Guppry, you're a Castolan, you don't think at all like a Halceen. Why did my good Halceen people follow you?"

A little smugly Guppry replied, "Sometimes it takes a stranger to see the truth and point it out. After that, anyone could see that they were being robbed by the nobles. They only had to look up toward the palace to see where their taxes went."

"You've been through the palace. Everything in it is five generations old. I spent almost nothing on the palace. The new cistern was about it."

"The dance floor in the pavilion—"

"That's new, yes, but a government has other expenses, Guppry. Salaries for officials, the army, cleaning crews and gardeners, prophets . . . That one I could have skipped."

"I bought your prophets, Sarol."

"They must be long gone by now, hey? They saw you'd win, and they saw what would follow. What I started to say was, a Halceen wouldn't be racking his wits for ways to stop a suicide. Suicide is a kind of last refuge."

"One you didn't take."

"But I *chose* not to. It was there for me. Guppry, I believe that's Zarop-Opar ahead."

The trees didn't thin out. They ended abruptly, where kings' oaths prevented mere woodcutters from crossing. Beyond, the path became a paved road that curved to the left around Mount Demonhead and ran to Zarop the capital.

Guppry asked a little maliciously, "Where do you go from here, Sarol?"

Sarol laughed. "I'd thought of climbing Mount Demonhead. For the view, you know." And he rode out of the trees, followed by his knights and his ladies and theirs. King's oaths didn't stop them; they were escorting a Zarop-Opar princess. Guppry's men stopped, and so did Guppry.

Sarol turned his horse. "There's a marvelous view of Halceen from Mount Demonhead. You can see the whole country. I'd like to see what happens there at sunset tomorrow."

"What do you mean?"

"When you looked over the edge, did you happen to catch sight of something big and serpent-shaped, golden in color?"

"I saw a cloud formation that—"

"Those taxes that so irritated my people. Part of that money, a good part, went to hunters. We needed a lot of meat, and a variety too, to feed him. We had to buy salt, too. We didn't spend that much money on the army, Guppry, because we didn't need a big army. Came a big army against us, we sent the Worm after it."

"Worm?"

"I won't give you his real name. He lives in a cave below the edge, most of the time. At night he comes up to take food from our arms, if we speak the rites

correctly. We never did get enough suicides. Before
King Charl came, the Worm used to come over the
edge to feed. He'd crack open bungalows to get at
what was in them, the way we break a melon open
. . . but King Charl stopped that. They made him
King for that."

"You're sworn not to seek vengeance, Sarol!"

"I know it. I don't need to seek anything. I don't
think we'll climb Mount Demonhead after all; we'll
want to be a good way from the edge. Good-bye, Guppry. Good luck."

In these lands of magic and fabulous beasts and
men who keep their oaths, strangers become delight-
fully gullible. A native of the edge countries can make
a fool of even the wisest outlander. Later he may listen to his common sense when a man of the world's
edge is speaking. But common sense is not a good
guide either.

The thing to remember is this. Some men are liars.

Of Guppry's forty men, not one had been of the
palace staff; none had lived on the edge itself. They
were frightened. They looked to Guppry. Mindful of
his new dignity, Guppry put a sneer on his face as he
turned to watch Sarol's retinue depart. "Our retired
King is a great liar," he said cheerfully.

Certainly a practical joke need not be considered
as *vengeance* . . .

Certainly Sarol's oath could have forced him to
give warning . . .

Distant laughter drifted back from Sarol's lords and
ladies. None were looking back. Considering their
load, the horses were making all good speed.

And Guppry turned back toward the edge, as Sarol
must have known he would, because Guppry had no
choice at all.

Cautionary
Tales

TALLER than a man, thinner than a man, with a long neck and eyes set wide apart in his head, the creature still resembled a man; and he had aged like a man. Cosmic rays had robbed his fur of color, leaving a gray-white ruff along the base of his skull and over both ears. His pastel-pink skin was deeply wrinkled and marked with darker blotches. He carried himself like something precious and fragile. He was coming across the balcony toward Gordon.

Gordon had brought a packaged lunch from the Embassy. He ate alone. The bubble-world was a great cylinder whose landscape curled up and over his head: yellow-and-scarlet parkland, slate-colored buildings that bulged at the top. Below the balcony, patterned stars streamed beneath several square miles of window. There were a dozen breeds of alien on the public balcony, at least two of which had to be pets or symbiotes of other aliens; and no humans but for Gordon. Gordon wondered if the ancient humanoid resented his staring . . . then stared in earnest as the creature stopped before his table. The alien said, "May I break your privacy?"

Gordon nodded; but that could be misinterpreted, so he said, "I'm glad of the company."

The alien carefully lowered himself until he

sat cross-legged across the table. He said, "I seek never to die."

Gordon's heart jumped into his throat. "I'm not sure what you mean," he said cautiously. "The Fountain of Youth?"

"I do not care what form it takes." The alien spoke the Trade Language well, but his strange throat added a castinetlike clicking. "Our own legend holds no fountain. When we learned to cross between stars we found the legend of immortality wherever there were thinking beings. Whatever their shape or size or intelligence, whether they make their own worlds or make only clay pots, they all tell the tales of people who live forever."

"It's hard not to wonder if they have some basis," Gordon encouraged him.

The alien's head snapped around, fast enough and far enough to break a man's neck. The prominent lumps bobbing in his throat were of alien shape: not Adam's apple, but someone else's. "It must be so. I have searched too long for it to be false. You, have you ever found clues to the secret of living forever?"

Gordon searched when he could, when his Embassy job permitted it. There had been rumors about the Ftokteek. Gordon had followed the rumors out of human space, toward the galactic core and the Ftokteek Empire, to this Ftokteek-dominated meeting place of disparate life forms, this cloud of bubble-worlds of varying gravities and atmospheres. Gordon was middle-aged now, and Sol was invisible even to orbiting telescopes, and the Ftokteek died like anyone else.

He said, "We've got the legends. Look them up in the Human Embassy library. Ponce de Leon, and Gilgamesh, and Orpheus, and Tithonus, and . . . every god we ever had lived forever, if he didn't die by violence, and some could heal from that. Some religions say that some part of us lives on after we die."

"I will go to your library tomorrow," the alien said

without enthusiasm. "Do you have no more than legends?"

"No, but . . . do other species tell cautionary tales?"

"I do not understand."

Gordon said, "Some of our legends say you wouldn't want to live forever. Tithonus, for instance. A goddess gave him the gift of living forever, but she forgot to keep him young. He withered into a lizard. Adam and Eve were exiled by God; he was afraid they'd learn the secret of immortality and be as good as Him. Orpheus tried to bring a woman back from the dead. Some of the stories say you can't get immortality, and some say you'd go insane with boredom."

The alien pondered. "The tale tellers disdain immortality because they cannot have it. Jealousy? Could immortal beings have walked among you once?"

Gordon laughed. "I doubt it. Was that what made you come to me?"

"I go to the worlds where many species meet. When I see a creature new to me, then I ask. Sometimes I can sense others like me, who want never to die."

Gordon looked down past the edge of the balcony, down through the great window at the banded Jovian planet that held this swarm of bubble-worlds in their orbits. He came here every day; small wonder that the alien had picked him out. He came because he would not eat with the others. They thought he was crazy. He thought of them as mayflies, with their attention always on the passing moment, and no thought for the future. He thought of himself as an ambitious mayfly; and he ate alone.

The alien was saying, "When I was young I looked for the secret among the most advanced species. The great interstellar empires, the makers of artificial worlds, the creatures who mine stars for elements and send ships through the universe seeking ever more knowledge, would build their own immortality. But they die as you and I die. Some races live longer than mine, but they all die."

"The Ftokteek have a computerized library the size

of a small planet," Gordon said. He meant to get there someday, if he lived. "It must know damn near everything."

The alien answered with a whispery chuckle. "No bigger than a moon is the Ftokteek library. It told me nothing I could use."

The banded world passed from view.

"Then I looked among primitives," the alien said, "who live closer to their legends. They die. When I thought to talk to their ghosts, there was nothing, though I used their own techniques. Afterward I searched the vicinities of the black holes and other strange pockets of the universe, hoping that there may be places where entropy reverses itself. I found nothing. I examined the mathematics that describe the universe. I have learned a score of mathematical systems, and none hold any hope of entropy reversal, natural or created."

Gordon watched stars pass below his feet. He said, "Relativity. We used to think that if you traveled faster than light, time would reverse itself."

"I know eight systems of traveling faster than light."

"Eight? What is there besides ours and the Ftokteek drive?"

"Six others. I rode them all, and always I arrived older. My time runs short. I never examined the quasars, and now I would not live to reach them. What else is left? I have been searching for fourteen thousand years—" The alien didn't notice when Gordon made a peculiar hissing sound. "—in our counting. Less in yours, perhaps. Our world huddles closer to a cooler sun than this. Our year is twenty-one million standard seconds."

"What are you saying? Ours is only thirty-one million—"

"My present age is three hundred thirty-six point seven billion standard seconds in the Ftokteek counting."

"Ten thousand Earth years. More!"

"Far too long. I never mated. None carry my genes. Now none ever will, unless I can grow young again. There is little time left."

"But *why?*"

The alien seemed startled. "Because it is not enough. Because I am afraid to die. Are you short-lived, then?"

"Yes," said Gordon.

"Well, I have traveled with short-lived companions. They die, I mourn. I need a companion with the strength of youth. My spacecraft is better than any you could command. You may benefit from my research. We breathe a similar air mixture, our bodies use the same chemistry, we search for the same treasure. Will you join my quest?"

"No."

"But . . . I sensed that you seek immortality. I am never wrong. Don't you feel it, the certainty that there is a way to thwart entropy, to live forever?"

"I used to think so," said Gordon.

In the morning he arranged passage home to Sol system. Ten thousand years wasn't enough . . . no lifetime was enough, unless you lived it in such a way as to make it enough.

A lot of my main characters have been two to three hundred years old and in the prime of health. What the heck, it's science fiction . . . but it's also a side effect of my own personality. I want to live a long time. I can't help it.

Rotating Cylinders and the Possibility of Global Causality Violation

This story has a catchy title. I stole it from a mathematics paper by Frank J. Tipler.

"THREE hundred years we've been at war," said Quifting, "and I have the means to end it. I can destroy the Hallane Regency." He seemed very pleased with himself, and not at all awed at being in the presence of the emperor of seventy worlds.

The aforementioned emperor said, "That's a neat trick. If you can't pull it off, you can guess what penalties I might impose. None of my generals would dare such a brag."

"Their tools are not mine." Quifting shifted in a valuable antique massage chair. He was small and round and completely hairless: the style of the nonaristocratic professional. He *should* have been overawed, and frightened. "I'm a mathematician. Would you agree that a time machine would be a useful weapon of war?"

"I would," said the emperor. "Or I'd take a faster-than-light starship, if you're offering miracles."

"I'm offering miracles," said Quifting, "but to the enemy."

The emperor wondered if Quifting was mad. Mad or not, he was hardly dangerous. The emperor was halfway around the planet from him, on the night side. His side of the meeting room was only a holographic projection, though Quifting wouldn't know that.

Half a dozen clerks and couriers had allowed this man to reach the emperor's ersatz presence. Why? Possibly Quifting had useful suggestions, but not necessarily. Sometimes they let an entertaining madman through, lest the emperor grow bored.

"It's a very old idea," Quifting said earnestly. "I've traced it back three thousand years, to the era when spaceflight itself was only a dream. I can demonstrate that a massive rotating cylinder, infinite in length, can be circled by closed timelike paths. It sees reasonable that a long but finite—"

"Wait. I must have missed something."

"Take a massive cylinder," Quifting said patiently, "and put a rapid spin on it. I can plot a course for a spacecraft that will bring it around the cylinder and back to its starting point in space *and time.*"

"Ah. A functioning time machine, then. Done with relativity, I expect. But must the cylinder be infinitely long?"

"I wouldn't think so. A long but finite cylinder ought to show the same behavior, except near the endpoints."

"And when you say you can demonstrate this . . ."

"To another mathematician. Otherwise I would not have been allowed to meet Your Splendor. In addition, there are historical reasons to think that the cylinder need not be infinite."

Now the emperor was jolted. "Historical? Really?"

"That's surprising, isn't it? But it's easy to design a time machine, given the Terching Effect. You know about the Terching Effect?"

"It's what makes a warship's hull so rigid," confirmed the emperor.

"Yes. The cylinder must be very strong to take the rotation without flying apart. Of course it would be enormously expensive to build. But others have tried it. The Six Worlds Alliance started one during the Free Trade period."

"Really?"

"We have the records. Archeology had them fifty years ago, but they had no idea what the construct was intended to do. Idiots." Quifting's scowl was brief. "Never mind. A thousand years later, during the One Race Wars, the Mao Buddhists started to build such a time machine out in Sol's cometary halo. Again, behind the Coal Sack is a long, massive cylinder, a quasi-Terching-Effect shell enclosing a neutronium core. We think an alien race called the Kchipreesee built it. The ends are flared, possibly to compensate for edge effects, and there are fusion rocket motors in orbit around it, ready for attachment to spin it up to speed."

"Did nobody ever finish one of these, ah, time machines?"

Quifting pounced on the word. "Nobody!" and he leaned forward, grinning savagely at the emperor. No, he was not awed. A mathematician rules his empire absolutely, and it is more predictable, easier to manipulate, than any universe an emperor would dare believe in. "The Six Worlds Alliance fell apart before their project was barely started. The Mao Buddhist attempt—well, you know what happened to Sol system during the One Race Wars. As for the Kchipreesee, I'm told that many generations of space travel killed them off through biorhythm upset."

"That's ridiculous."

"It may be, but they are certainly extinct, and they certainly left their artifact half-finished."

"I don't understand," the emperor admitted. He was tall, muscular, built like a middleweight boxer. Health was the mark of aristocracy in this age. "You seem to be saying that building a time machine is simple but expensive, that it would handle any number of ships— It would, wouldn't it?"

"Oh, yes."

"—and send them back in time to exterminate one's enemies' ancestors. Others have tried it. But in practice, the project is always interrupted or abandoned."

"Exactly."

"Why?"

"Do you believe in cause and effect?"

"Of course. I . . . suppose that means I don't believe in time travel, doesn't it?"

"A working time machine would destroy the cause and effect relationship of the universe. It seems the universe resists such meddling. No time machine had ever been put into working condition. If the Hallane Regency tries it something will stop them. The Coal Sack is in Hallane space. They need only attach motors to the Kchipreesee device and spin it up."

"Bringing bad luck down upon their foolish heads. *Hubris.* The pride that challenges the gods. I like it. Yes. Let me see . . ." The emperor generally left war to his generals, but he took a high interest in espionage. He tapped at a pocket computer and said, "Get me Director Chilbreez."

To Quifting he said, "The director doesn't always arrest enemy spies. Sometimes he just watches 'em. I'll have him pick one and give him a lucky break, Let him stumble on a vital secret, as it were."

"You'd have to back it up—"

"Ah, but we're already trying to recapture Coal Sack space. We'll step up the attacks a little. We should be able to convince the Hallanes that we're trying to take away their time machine. Even if you're completely wrong—which I suspect is true—we'll have them wasting some of their industrial capacity. Maybe start some factional disputes, too. Pro- and anti-time-machine. Hah!" The emperor's smile suddenly left him. "Suppose they actually build a time machine?"

"They won't."

"But a time machine is possible? The mathematics works?"

"But that's the point, Your Splendor. The universe

itself resists such things." Quifting smiled confidently. "Don't you believe in cause and effect?"

"Yes."

Violet-white light blazed through the windows behind the mathematician making of him a sharp-edged black shadow. Quifting ran forward and smashed into the holograph wall. His eyes were shut tight, his clothes were afire. "What is it?" he screamed. "What's happening?"

"I imagine the sun has gone nova," said the emperor. The wall went black.

A dulcet voice spoke. "Director Chilbreez on the line."

"Never mind." There was no point now in telling the director how to get an enemy to build a time machine. The universe protected its cause-and-effect basis with humorless ferocity. Director Chilbreez was doomed; and perhaps Quifting had ended the war after all. The emperor went to the window. A churning aurora blazed bright as day, and grew brighter still.

Plomething

THE children were playing six-point Overlord, hopping from point to point over a hexagonal diagram drawn in the sand, when the probe broke atmosphere over their heads. They might have sensed it then, for it was heating fast as it entered atmosphere; but nobody happened to look up.

Seconds later the retrorocket fired.

A gentle rain of infrared light bathed the limonite sands. Over hundreds of square miles of orange martian desert, wide-spaced clumps of black grass uncurled their leaves to catch and hoard the heat. Tiny sessile things buried beneath the sand raised fan-shaped probes.

The children hadn't noticed yet, but their ears were stirring. Their ears sensed heat rather than sound; and unless they were listening to some heat source, they usually remained folded against the children's heads, like silver flowers. Now they uncurled, flowers blooming, showing black centers; now they twitched and turned, seeking. One turned and saw it.

A point of white light high in the east, slowly setting.

The children talked to each other in coded pulses of heat, opening and closing their mouths to show the warm interiors.

Hey!

What is it?
Let's go see!

They hopped off across the limonite sand, forgetting the Overlord game, racing to meet the falling thing.

It was down when they got there, and still shouting-hot. The probe was big, as big as a dwelling, a fat cylinder with a rounded roof above and a great hot mouth beneath. Black and white paint in a checker-board pattern made it look like a giant's toy. It rested on three comically splayed metal legs with wide circular feet.

The children began rubbing against the metal skin, flashing pulses of contentment as they felt the heat.

The probe trembled. Motion inside. The children jumped back, stood looking at each other, each ready to run if the others did. None wanted to be first. Suddenly it was too late. One whole curved wall of the probe dropped outward and thudded to the sand.

A child crawled out from underneath, rubbing his head and flashing heat from his mouth: words he shouldn't have learned yet. The wound in his scalp steamed briefly before the edges pulled shut.

The small, intense white sun, halfway down the sky, cast opaque black shadow across the opening in the probe. In the shadow something stirred.

The children watched, awed.

ABEL paused in the opening, then rolled out, using the slab of reentry shielding as a ramp. ABEL was a cluster of plastic and metal widgetry mounted on a low platform slung between six balloon tires. When it reached the sand it hesitated as if uncertain, then rolled out onto Mars, jerkily, feeling its way.

The child who'd been bumped by the ramp hopped over to kick the moving thing. ABEL stopped at once. The child shied back.

Suddenly an adult stood among them.

WHAT ARE YOU DOING?

Nothing, one answered.

Just playing, said another.

WELL, BE CAREFUL WITH IT. The adult looked like a twin to any of the six children. The roof of his mouth was warmer than theirs, but the authority in his voice was due to more than mere loudness. *SOME-ONE MAY HAVE GONE TO GREAT TROUBLE TO BUILD THIS OBJECT.*

Yes sir.

Somewhat subdued, the children gathered around the Automated Biological Laboratory. They watched a door open in the side of the drum-shaped container that made up half of ABEL's body. A gun inside the door fired a weighted line high into the air.

That thing almost hit me.

Serves you right.

The line, coated with sand dust, came slithering back into ABEL's side. One of the children licked it and found it covered with something sticky and taste-less.

Two children climbed onto the slow-moving plat-form, then up onto the cylinder. They stood up and waved their arms, balancing precariously on flat tri-angular feet. ABEL swerved toward a clump of black grass, and both children toppled to the sand. One picked himself up and ran to climb on again.

The adult watched it all dubiously.

A second adult appeared beside him.

YOU ARE LATE. WE HAD AN APPOINT-MENT TO XAT BNORNEN CHIP. HAD YOU FORGOTTEN?

I HAD. THE CHILDREN HAVE FOUND SOMETHING.

SO THEY HAVE. WHAT IS IT DOING?

IT WAS TAKING SOIL SAMPLES AND PER-HAPS TRYING TO COLLECT SPORES. NOW IT SHOWS AN INTEREST IN GRASS. I WONDER HOW ACCURATE ARE ITS INSTRUMENTS.

IF IT WERE SENTIENT IT WOULD SHOW IN-TEREST IN THE CHILDREN.

PERHAPS.

ABEL stopped. A box at the front lifted on a telescoping leg and began a slow pan of the landscape. From the low dark line of the Mare Acidalium highlands on the northeastern horizon, it swung around until its lens faced straight backward, at the empty orange desert of Tractus Albus. At this point the lens was eye to eye with the hitchhiking child. The child flapped his ears, made idiot faces, shouted nonsense words, and flicked at the lens with his long tongue.

THAT SHOULD GIVE THEM SOMETHING TO THINK ABOUT.

WHO WOULD YOU SAY SENT IT?

EARTH, I WOULD THINK. NOTICE THE SILICATE DISC IN THE CAMERA, TRANSPARENT TO THE FREQUENCIES OF LIGHT MOST LIKELY TO PENETRATE THE PLANET'S THICK ATMOSPHERE.

AGREEMENT.

The gun fired again, into the black grass, and the line began to reel back. Another box retracted its curved lid. The hitchhiker peered into it, while the other children watched admiringly from below.

One of the adults shouted, *GET BACK, YOU YOUNG PLANTBRAIN!*

The child turned to flap his ears at him. At that moment ABEL flashed a tight ruby beam of laser light just past his ear. For an instant it showed, an infinite length of neon tubing against the navy blue sky.

The child scrambled down and ran for his life.

EARTH IS NOT IN THAT DIRECTION, an adult observed.

YET THE BEAM MUST HAVE BEEN A MESSAGE. SOMETHING IN ORBIT, PERHAPS?

The adults looked skyward. Presently their eyes adjusted.

ON THE INNER MOON. DO YOU SEE IT?

YES. QUITE LARGE . . . AND WHAT ARE THOSE MIDGES IN MOTION ABOUT IT? THAT IS NO AUTOMATED PROBE. BUT A VEHICLE. I THINK WE MUST EXPECT VISITORS SOON.

WE SHOULD HAVE INFORMED THEM OF

OUR PRESENCE LONG AGO. A LARGE RADIO FREQUENCY LASER WOULD HAVE DONE IT. WHY SHOULD WE DO ALL THE WORK WHEN THEY HAVE ALL THE METALS, THE SUNLIGHT, THE RESOURCES?

Having finished with the clump of grass, ABEL lurched into motion and rolled toward a dark line of eroded ring wall. The children swarmed after it. The lab fired off another sticky string, let it fall, and started to reel it back. A child picked it up and pulled. Lab and martian engaged in a tug of war which ended when the string broke. Another child poked a long, fragile finger into the cavity and withdrew it covered with something wet. Before it could boil away, he put the finger in his mouth. He sent out a pulse of pleasure and stuck his tongue in the hole, into the broth intended for growing martian microorganisms.

STOP THAT! THAT IS NOT YOUR PROPERTY!

The adult voice was ignored. The child left his tongue in the broth, running alongside the lab to keep up. Presently the others discovered that if they stood in front of ABEL, it would change course to crawl around the "obstruction."

PERHAPS THE ALIENS WILL BE SATISFIED TO RETURN HOME WITH THE INFORMATION GATHERED BY THE PROBE.

NONSENSE. THE CAMERAS HAVE SEEN THE CHILDREN. NOW THEY KNOW THAT WE EXIST.

WOULD THEY RISK THEIR LIVES TO LAND, MERELY BECAUSE THEY HAVE SEEN DITHTA? DITHTA IS A HOMELY CHILD, EVEN TO MY OWN EYE, AND I AM PERHAPS HIS PARENT.

LOOK WHAT THEY ARE DOING NOW.

By moving to left and right of the lab, by forming moving "obstructions," the children were steering ABEL toward a cliff. One still rode high on top, pretending to steer by kicking the metal flanks.

WE MUST STOP THEM. THEY WILL BREAK IT.

YES . . . DO YOU REALLY EXPECT THAT THE ALIENS WILL LAND A MANNED VEHICLE?

IT IS THE OBVIOUS NEXT STEP.

WE MUST HOPE THAT THE CHILDREN WILL NOT GET HOLD OF IT.

Mistake

IN a cargo craft between Earth and Ganymede, Commander Elroy Barnes lolled in his crash couch with a silly smile on his face. The shovel-blade re-entry shield was swung down from the ship's nose, exposing the cabin's great curved window. Barnes watched the unwinking stars. It was a few minutes before he noticed the alien staring in at him.

He studied it. Eight feet tall, roughly reptilian, with a scaly, domed head and a mouth furnished with several dozen polished stiletto-blade teeth. Its hands were four-fingered claws, and one held a wide-barreled pistol-like tool.

Barnes lifted a languid hand and waved.

Kthistlmup was puzzled. The human's mind was muzzy, almost unreadable. The alien probed the ship for other minds, but the ship was empty save for Barnes.

Kthistlmup stepped through the glass into the cabin.

Barnes showed surprise for the first time. "Hey, that was neat! Do it again."

"There's something wrong with you," Kthistlmup projected.

Barnes grinned. "Certain measures are necessary to combat the boredom of space, to s-safeguard the sanity of our pilots." He lifted a green plastic pill bottle.

"NST-24. Makes for a good trip. Nothing to do out here till I have to guide the beast into the Jupiter system. So why not?"

"Why not what?"

"Why not take a little trip while I take the big one?"

Kthistlmup understood at last. "You've done something to your mind. Chemicals? We use direct-current stimulus on Mars."

"Mars? Are you really—"

"Barnes, I must ask you questions."

Barnes waved expansively. "Shoot."

"How well is Earth prepared against an attack from space?"

"That's a *secret*. Besides, I don't have the vaguest notion."

"You must have some notion. What's the most powerful weapon you ever heard of?"

Barnes folded his arms. "Won't say." His mind showed only a blaze of white light, which might not have anything to do with the question.

Kthistlmup tried again. "Has Earth colonized other planets?"

"Sure. Trantor, Mesklin, Barsoom, Perelandra . . ."

Barnes' mind showed only that he was lying, and Kthistlmup had lost patience. "You will answer," he said, and reached forward to take Barnes' throat delicately between four needle-sharp claws.

Barnes' eyes grew large. "Oh, oh, bad trip! Gimme, gimme the bottle of Ends! Quick!"

Kthistlmup let go. "Tell me about Earth's defenses."

"I got to have an End. Big blue bottle, it should be in the medicine chest." Barnes reached to the side. He had the wall cabinet open before Kthistlmup caught his wrist.

"This 'End.' What will it do?"

"End the trip. Fix me up."

"It will clear your mind?"

"Right."

Kthistlmup released him. He watched as Barnes swallowed an oval pill, dry.

"It's for in case we're going to run across an asteroid, so I can recompute the course fast," Barnes explained.

Kthistlmup watched as Barnes' mind began to clear. In a minute Barnes would be unable to hide his thoughts. It wouldn't matter if he answered or not. Kthistlmup need only read the pictures his questions produced.

Barnes' mind cleared further . . . and Kthistlmup found himself fading out of existence. His last thought was that it had been a perfectly natural mistake.

Night on
Mispec Moor

IN predawn darkness the battle began to take shape. Helicopters circled, carrying newstapers and monitors. Below, the two armies jockeyed for position. They dared not meet before dawn. The monitors would declare a mistrial and fine both sides heavily.

In the red dawn the battle began. Scout groups probed each other's skills. The weapons were identical on both sides: heavy swords with big basket hilts. Only the men themselves differed in skill and strength.

By noon the battle had concentrated on a bare plain strewn with white boulders and a few tight circles of green Seredan vegetation. The warriors moved in little clumps. Where they met, the yellow dirt was stained red, and cameras in the helicopters caught it all for public viewing.

Days were short on Sereda. For some, today was not short enough.

As Sereda's orange dwarf sun dropped toward the horizon, the battle had become a massacre with the Greys at the wrong end. When Tomás Vatch could no longer hold a sword, he ran. Other Greys had fled, and Amber soldiers streamed after them, yelling. Vatch ran with blood flowing down his sword arm and dripping from his fingertips. He was falling behind, and the Ambers were coming close.

He turned sharp left and kept running. The swarm moved north, toward the edge of Mispec Moor, toward civilization. Alone, he had a chance. The Ambers would not concern themselves with a single fleeing man.

But one did. One golden-skinned red-haired man shouted something, waved his sword in a circle over his head, and followed.

An ancient glacier had dropped blocks of limestone and granite all over this flat, barren region. The biggest rock in sight was twice the height of a man and wider than it was tall. Vatch ran toward it. He had not yet begun to wonder how he would climb it.

He moved in a quick unbalanced stumble now, his sword and his medical kit bouncing awkwardly at either side. He had dropped the sword once already, when a blade had sliced into him just under the armpit. The heavy-shouldered warrior had paused to gloat, and Vatch had caught the falling sword in his left hand and jabbed upward. Now he cradled his right arm in his left to keep it from flopping loose.

He'd reached the rock.

It was split wide open down the middle.

The red-haired Amber came on like an exuberant child. Vatch had noticed him early in the battle. He'd fought that way too, laughing and slashing about him with playful enthusiasm. Vatch thought his attitude inappropriate to so serious a matter as war.

Vatch stepped into the mammoth crack, set his back to one side and his feet to the other, and began to work his way up. Recent wounds opened, and blood flowed down the rock. Vatch went on, concentrating on the placement of his feet, trying not to wonder what would happen if the Amber caught him halfway up.

The red-haired man arrived, blowing and laughing, and found Vatch high above him. He reached up with his sword. Vatch, braced awkwardly between two lips of granite, felt the sharp tip poking him in the small of the back. The Amber was standing on tiptoe; he could reach no further.

The top was flat. Vatch rolled over on his belly and rested. The world whirled around him. He had lost much blood.

And he couldn't afford this. He forced himself to sit up and look around. Where was the enemy?

A rock whizzed past his head. A voice bellowed, "Rammer! Give my regards to the nightwalkers!"

Vatch heard running footsteps, fading. He stood up.

Omicron 2 Eridani was a wide, distorted red blob on the flat horizon. Vatch could see far across Mispec Moor. He found his erstwhile enemy jogging north. Far ahead of him swarmed the army of the Ambers. Above them, the helicopters were bright motes.

Vatch smiled and dropped back to prone position. He was safe. No man, woman or child of Sereda would stay at night upon Mispec Moor.

On Sereda war is a heavily supervised institution. Battles are fought with agreed-upon weaponry. Strategy lies in getting the enemy to agree to the right weapons. This day the Greys had been out-strategied. The Ambers had the better swordsmen.

Seredan war set no limits to the use of medicine, provided that nothing in a medical kit could be used as a weapon, and provided that all medicines must be carried by fighting men. The convention was advantageous to an outworld mercenary.

Vatch fumbled the medical kit open, one-handed. He suspected that the gathering darkness was partly in his own eyes. But the Spectrum Cure was there: a soft plastic bottle, half-liter size, with a spray hypo and a pistol grip attached. Vatch pressure-injected himself, put the bottle carefully away and let himself roll over on his back.

The first effect was a tingling all through him.

Then his wounds stopped bleeding.

Then they closed.

His fatigue began to recede.

Vatch smiled up at the darkening sky. He'd be paid high for this day's work. His sword arm wasn't very good; he'd thought that Sereda's lower gravity would make a mighty warrior of him, but that hadn't worked out. But this Spectrum Cure was tremendous stuff! The biochemists of Miramon Lluagor had formulated it. It was ten years old there, and brand new on Sereda, and the other worlds of the Léshy circuit probably hadn't even heard of it yet. At the start of the battle he'd had enough to inject forty men, to heal them of any wound or disease, as long as their hearts still beat to distribute the stuff. The bottle was two-thirds empty now. He'd done a fair day's work, turning casualties back into fighting men while the battle raged about him.

The only adverse effect of Spectrum Cure began to show itself. Hunger. His belly was a yawning pit. Healing took metabolic energy. Tomás Vatch sat up convulsively and looked about him.

The damp air of Sereda was turning to mist around the foot of the rock.

He let himself over the lip, hung by his fingertips, and dropped. His belly was making grinding noises and sending signals of desperation. He had not eaten since early this morning. He set off at a brisk walk toward the nearest possible source of dinner: the battleground.

Twilight was fading rapidly. The mist crept over the ground like a soggy blanket. There were patches of grass-green on the yellow dirt, far apart, each several feet across and sharply bordered, each with a high yellow-tipped stalk springing from the center. The mist covered these too. Soon Vatch could see only a few blossoms like frilly yellow morels hovering at waist level, and shadowy white boulders looming like ghosts around him. His passage set up swirling currents.

Like most of the rammers, the men who travel the worlds of the Léshy circuit, Vatch had read the fantasies of James Branch Cabell. The early interstellar scout who discovered these worlds four hundred years ago had read Cabell. Toupan, Miramon Lluagor, Sereda, Horvendile, Koschei: the powerful though mortal Léshy of Cabell's fantasies had become five worlds circling five suns in a bent ring, with Earth and Sol making a sixth. Those who settled the Léshy worlds had followed tradition in the naming of names. A man who had read Cabell could guess the nature of a place from its name alone.

The Mispec Moor of Cabell's writings had been a place of supernatural mystery, a place where reality was vague and higher realities showed through.

Mispec Moor on Sereda had just that vague look, with darkness falling over waist-high mist and shadowy boulders looming above; and Vatch now remembered that this Mispec Moor had a complimentary set of legends. Sereda's people did not call them vampires or ghouls, but the fearsome nightwalkers of Mispec Moor seemed a combination of the two legends: things that had been men, whose bite would turn living or dead alike into more nightwalkers. They could survive ordinary weapons, but a silver bullet would stop them, especially if it had been dumdummed by a cross cut into its nose.

Naturally Tomás Vatch carried no silver bullets and no gun. He was lucky to be carrying a flashlight. He had not expected to be out at night, but the flashlight was part of his kit. He had often needed light to perform his secondary battlefield duties.

As he neared the place of the fallen soldiers he thought he saw motion in the mist. He raised the flashlight high over his head and drew his sword.

Thin shapes scampered away from the light. Tomás jumped violently—and then he recognized lopers, the doglike scavengers of Sereda. He kept his sword in hand. The lopers kept their distance, and he let them be. They were here for the same reason he was, he thought with no amusement at all.

Some soldiers carried bread or rolls of hard candy into battle.

Some of these never ate their provisions.

It was a repugnant task, this searching of dead men. He found the body of Robroy Tanner, who had come with him to Sereda aboard a Lluagorian ramship; and he cried, out here where nobody could see him. But he continued to search. He was savagely hungry.

The lopers had been at some of the bodies. More than once he was tempted to end his whimsical truce. The lopers still moved at the periphery of his vision. They seemed shy of the light, but would that last? Certainly the legends pointed to something dangerous on Mispec Moor. Could the lopers themselves be subject to something like rabies?

He found hard candy, and he found two canteens, both nearly empty. He sucked the candy a roll at a time, his cheeks puffed out like a squirrel's. Presently he found the slashed corpse of a man he had eaten breakfast with. *Jackpot.* He had watched Erwin Mudd take a block of stew from a freezer and double-wrap it in plastic bags, just before they entered the battle-field.

The stew was there. Vatch ate it as it was, cold, and was grateful for it.

Motion in the mist made him look up.

Two shadows were coming toward him. They were much bigger than lopers . . . and man-shaped.

Vatch stood up and called, "Hello?"

They came on, taking shape as they neared. A third blurred shadow congealed behind them. They had not answered. Annoyed, Vatch swung the flash-light beam toward them.

The light caught them full. Vatch held it steady, staring, not believing. Then, still not believing, he screamed and ran.

There is a way a healthy man can pace himself so that he can jog for hours across flat land, especially on a low-gravity world like Sereda. Tomás Vatch had that skill.

But now he ran like a mad sprinter, in sheer panic,

his chest heaving, his legs burning. It was a minute or so before he thought to turn off the flashlight so that the things could not follow its glow. It was much longer before he could work up the courage to look back.

One of the things was following him.

He did not think to stand and fight. He had seen it too clearly. It was a corpse, weeks dead. He thought of turning toward the city, but the city was a good distance away; and now he remembered that they locked the gates at night. The first time he had seen them do that, he had asked why, and a native policeman had told him of the nightwalkers. He had had to hear the story from other sources before he knew that he was not being played for a gullible outworlder.

So he did not turn toward the city. He turned toward the rock that had been his refuge once before.

The thing followed. It moved at a fast walk; but, where Tomás Vatch had to stop and rest with his hands on his knees to catch his breath before he ran on, the nightwalker never stopped at all. It was a distant shadow when he reached the rock; but his haste was such that he skinned his shoulders working himself up the crack.

The top of the rock was still warm from daylight. Vatch lay on his back and felt the joy of breathing. The stars were clear and bright above him. There was no sound at all.

But when his breathing quieted he heard heavy, uneven footsteps.

He looked over the edge of the rock.

The nightwalker came wading through the mist in a wobbling shuffle. It walked like it would fall down at every step, and its feet fell joltingly hard. Yet it came fast. Its bulging eyes stared back into Vatch's flashlight.

Why should a nightwalker care if it sprained its ankles at every step? It was dead, dead and bloated. It still wore a soldier's kilt in green plaid, the sign of a commercial war now two weeks old. Above the broad belt a slashed belly wound gaped wide.

Vatch examined the corpse with self-conscious care. The only way he knew to quell his panic was to put his mind to work. He searched for evidence that this nightwalker was not what it seemed, that it was something else, a native life form, say, with a gift for mimickry.

It stood at the base of the rock, looking up with dull eyes and slack mouth. A walking dead man.

There was more motion in the mist . . . and two lopers came lurching up to stand near the nightwalker. When Vatch threw the light on them they stared back unblinking. Presently Vatch realized why. They, too, were dead.

The policeman had told him that too: that nightwalkers could take the form of lopers and other things.

He had believed very little of what he had heard . . . and now he was trying frantically to remember details. They were not dangerous in daytime; hadn't he heard that? Then if he could hold out here till morning, he would be safe. He could return to the city.

But three more man-shapes were coming to join the first.

And the first was clawing at the side of the rock, trying to find purchase for its fingers. It moved along the base, scraping at the rough side. It entered the crack . . .

Three shadows came out of the mist to join their brother. One wore the familiar plaid kilt from that two-week-old battle. One wore a businessman's tunic; its white hair had come away in patches, taking scalp with it. The third had been a small, slender woman, judging from her dress and her long yellow hair.

They clawed at the rock. They began to spread out along the base.

And Vatch backed away from the edge and sat down.

What the hell was this? Legends like this had been

left behind on Earth! Dead men did not walk, not without help. Ordinarily they just *lay* there. What was different about Sereda? What kind of biology could fit—? Vatch shook his head violently. The question was nonsense. This was fantasy, and he was in it.

Yet his mind clutched for explanations:

Costumes? Suppose a group of Seredans had something to hide out here. (What?) A guard of four in dreadful costumes might hold off a whole city, once the legend of the nightwalker was established (But the legend was a century old. Never mind, the legend could have come first.) Anyone who came close enough to see the fraud could quietly disappear. (Costume and makeup? That gaping putrescent belly wound!)

Out of the crack in the rock came a fantasy arm, the bone showing through the forearm, the first joints missing on all the ragged fingers. Vatch froze. (*Costume?*) The other arm came up, and then a dead slack face. The smell reached him . . .

Vatch unfroze very suddenly, snatched up his sword and struck overhand. He split the skull to the chin.

The nightwalker was still trying to pull itself up.

Vatch struck at the arms. He severed one elbow, then the other, and the nightwalker dropped away without a cry.

Vatch began to shudder. He couldn't stop the spasms; he could only wait until they passed. He was beginning to understand how the fantasy would end. When the horror became too great, when he could stand it no longer, he would leap screaming to the ground and try to kill them all. And his sword would not be enough.

It was real! The dead forearms lay near his feet!

Fantasy!

Real!

Wait, wait. A fantasy was something that categorically could not happen. It was *always* a story, *always* something that originated in a man's mind. Could he be starring in somebody's fantasy?

This, a form of entertainment? Then it had holovision beat hands down. But Vatch knew of no world that had the technology to create such a total-experience entertainment, complete with what had to be ersatz memories! No world had that, let alone backward Sereda!

Wait. Was he really on Sereda? Was the date really 2731? Or was he living through some kind of Gothic historical?

Was he even Tomás Vatch the rammer? Rammer was a high-prestige career. Someone might well have paid for the illusion that he was a rammer . . . and if he had, someone had gotten more than he had bargained for. They'd pull him out of his total-environment cubical or theater in total catatonic withdrawal, if Tomás Vatch didn't get a grip on himself.

Wait. Was that motion in the mist, off toward the battlefield?

Or more of his runaway imagination? But no, the mist was a curdling, swirling line, aimed at his rock.

That almost did it. He almost leapt from the rock and ran. If the city gates were closed he'd run right up the walls . . . But he waited. In a minute he'd know for sure, one way or another.

Within the crack the one he had struck sat slumped with its head bowed, disconsolate or truly dead. The other three seemed to be accomplishing very little.

The dead men from the battlefield streamed toward Vatch's place of refuge. They wore kilts of grey and amber. Less than a hundred of them, casualties in a war between two medium-sized companies, a war which would not have been fought at all if the cost could not be partly defrayed by holovision rights. When they came close Vatch began to recognize individuals. There was Erwin Mudd, whose stew he had stolen. There was Roy Tanner the Lluagorian, the rammer, the medic. Death cancels all friendships. There— Enough. *Forget about costumes, Tomás.*

Enough, and too late. The nightwalkers swarmed around the rock and began trying to climb. Vatch stood above the crack, sword ready. The sword was all he had.

Hands came over the edge. He struck at them.

He looked around in time to see more hands coming up everywhere along the perimeter. He yelled and circled madly, striking, striking. They were not climbing the rock itself; they were climbing over each other to reach the top. And his sword, its edge dulled by repeated blows against rock and bone, was turning into a club . . .

Suddenly he stopped.

Fantasy? Real? What kind of biology . . . ?

He spilled his medical kit open and snatched at the bottle of Spectrum Cure. More than his life was at stake here. He was trying to save his sanity.

The pistol grip fitted his hand neatly. A nightwalker pulled itself over the edge and tottered toward him, and he sprayed Spectrum Cure between its eyes. An eroded face appeared near his feet; he sprayed Spectrum Cure into its mouth. Then he stepped back and watched.

The first one dropped like a sack. The second let go and disappeared from view.

Nightwalkers were coming up all around him. Vatch moved among them in calm haste, spraying life into them, and they stopped moving. In his mind he gloated. It should have worked, and it had.

For if anything in this experience was real, then it had to be caused by the biology of Sereda. So: something could infect the dead, to make them move. Bacterium? Fungus? Virus? Whatever it was, it had to have evolved by using dead lopers and other native life forms to spread itself.

It would walk the infected corpse until there was no sugar or oxygen left in the blood or muscle tissues of the host. That alone could carry the disease further than it could travel by itself. And if it found another host to infect along the way, well and good.

But the first step in infection would be to restart the heart. It *had* to be, or the bacterium couldn't spread throughout the host.

And if the heart was going . . .

The Spectrum Cure seemed to be healing them right up. He'd cured about eight of them. They lay at the base of the rock and did not move. Other nightwalkers clustered around them. For the moment they had given up on Vatch's rock.

Vatch watched some of them bend over the bodies of those he had injected. They might have been nibbling at the flesh above the hearts. A minute of that, and then they fell over and lay as dead as the ones they had been trying to rescue.

Good enough, thought Vatch. He flashed the light on his bottle to check the supply of Spectrum Cure.

It was just short of dead empty.

Vatch sighed. The horde of dead men had drawn away from the casualties—the *dead* dead ones—and gone back to trying to climb the rock. Some would make it. Vatch picked up his sword. An afterthought: he injected himself. Even if they got to him, they would not rouse him from death before morning.

The scrabbling of finger bones against rock became a cricket chorus.

Vatch stood looking down at them. Most of these had only been dead for hours. Their faces were intact, though slack. Vatch looked for Roy Tanner.

He circled the edge rapidly, striking occasionally at a reaching arm, but peering down anxiously. Where the blazes was Roy Tanner?

There, pulling himself over the lip of the crack.

In fact they were all swarming into the crack and climbing over each other. Their dead brains must be working to some extent. The smell of them was terrific. Vatch breathed through his mouth, closed his imagination tight shut, and waited.

The nightwalker remains of Roy Tanner pulled itself up on the rock. Vatch sprayed it in the face, turned the body over in haste, and found it: Roy Tanner's medical kit, still intact. He spilled out the contents and snatched up Roy's bottle of Spectrum Cure.

He sprayed it before him, and then into the crack, like an insecticide. He held his aim until they stopped moving . . . and then, finally, he could roll away from the choking smell. It was all right now. Roy had fallen early in the battle. His bottle had been nearly full.

For something like six hours they had watched each other: Tomás Vatch on the lip of the rock, seven nightwalkers below. They stood in a half circle, well out of range of Vatch's spray gun, and they stared unblinking into Vatch's flashlight.

Vatch was dreadfully tired. He had circled the rock several times, leaping the crack twice on each pass. "Cured" corpses surrounded the base and half filled the crack. He had seen none of them move. By now he was sure. There were only these seven left.

"I want to sleep," he told them. "Can't you understand? I won. You lost. Go away. I want to sleep." He had been telling them this for some time.

This time it seemed that they heard.

One by one they turned and stumbled off in different directions. Vatch watched, amazed, afraid to believe. Each nightwalker seemed to find a patch of level ground it liked. There it fell and did not move.

Vatch waited. The east was growing bright. It wasn't over yet, but it would be soon. With burning eyes he watched for the obvious dead to move again.

Red dawn touched the tips of glacier-spilled rocks. The orange dwarf sun made a cool light; he could almost look straight into it. He watched the shadows walk down the sides of the rocks to the ground.

When the light touched the seven bodies, they had become bright green patches, vaguely man-shaped.

Vatch watched until each patch had sprouted a bud of yellow in its center. Then he dropped to the ground and started walking north.

Wrong Way
Street

"Wrong Way Street" has never been in any of my collections; but it has been in a *Galaxy* "best" anthology, and an anthology of time-travel stories, and a theme collection of "first man on the Moon" stories. More success than I expected for my second professional sale. Naturally I remember the story with fondness. I sometimes wish I could write more about the critters who built that peculiar base on the Moon . . . but of course there's no way.

———

MIKE Capoferri turned out to be at one time in his life the loneliest man on the Moon. But it was not his first venture into aloneness. He had felt it before, almost twenty years before, when he was twelve and his eight-year-old brother died.

Young Tony had been riding a Flexy, a kind of bobsled on wheels, down the hill road above Venice Boulevard. At the bottom of the hill he had turned hard right onto Venice. The Flexy had flipped over on its back, and its blunt rubber handle had poked hard into Tony's stomach.

One of the first things the doctor did was to take Tony's blood pressure. It was low, which meant shock. It started to fall almost as soon as the blood pressure cuff was removed, but the doctor didn't know that until it was too late. Tony's spleen was ruptured.

Mike had loved his younger brother. He sat in his room most of the time, unable to get used to his loss, and not really trying. After four weeks of it his father neglected his own grief long enough to take Mike to a child psychologist.

Mike was a recent but ardent science fiction fan. "I want to change it, Doctor Stuart," he said earnestly. "I want to go back to four weeks ago and take away Tony's Flexy." He meant it, of course.

Doctor Stuart had worked hard to get Mike to say those words. If he was thinking in terms of sibling rivalries and guilt feelings, it didn't show. "You can't do that, Mike. Time is a one-way street with no parking spaces. You just have to keep going."

"Until you have an accident," Mike said bitterly.

Doctor Stuart nodded. "Or run out of gas," he added, because he himself was old enough for the analogy to apply. They talked for almost three hours, with Mike doing most of the talking. Afterward Mike gradually stopped mourning.

When Mike Capoferri graduated from high school he had become intensely interested in space travel. His first year at Cal Tech was the year Walnikov landed on Mars. Mike was determined to follow.

In a way he traveled further than Walnikov. He never got to Mars, but he did make it to the Moon. And unlike Mars, the Moon once had intelligent visitors.

Mike was one of many. Thirty men and women had come to the alien base, determined to probe all its secrets. By this time Mike was thirty-one years old and held doctorates in physics, mathematics and philosophy. He was tall, dark, not too homely, a little too earnest. He got over that at the base, where the only defense against strangeness was a sense of humor.

Besides the base, the aliens had thoughtfully provided one spaceship. It rested on its side near the base, a fat cylinder with conical ends and asymmetrical bulges in unexpected places. Mike began going through the ship before he ever entered the base, and he kept at it through the years. This wasn't unusual. The ship was thought to be the real treasure, for its star charts showed (in hard-to-read notations in ultraviolet ink) that it had cruised between widely separated stars. It may have had a faster-than-light drive.

The base personnel lived in the base itself, with their own air regenerating system and their own airlock built into the open alien airlock. There was plenty of room for them. The aliens had averaged ten feet tall, and there were things which must have been bunks for forty-eight of them.

Still, the base took getting used to. The alien engineers had put steps and ledges in the floor wherever the ground beneath wasn't exactly level. Newcomers learned not to sit on the "bunks," which looked like pieces of free-form sculpture, felt like foam rubber with a metal core, and changed shape without warning. They were told not to touch mosaic designs which had been marked with paint, for the design might hide a control of some kind.

It was four years since Mike had landed on the Moon. In that time the human tenants had made a great deal of progress.

An emergency repair kit from the ship had yielded a method of creating artificial crystals of almost any shape from almost any solid, by building them up atom by atom. Already ships had lifted on rocket motors built from large diamonds.

A box which held perfectly preserved sections from some non-terrestrial animals, possibly used as food, had given them a field which would interrupt any chemical process. The applications were numerous and varied. A short-range death ray. A beam to fight forest fires. A new method of inducing suspended animation, very useful in surgery.

A sculpting implement, used by the aliens as a

means of recreation (the base was infested with the statues they had left behind), had become a disintegrator. Turning it on had been heartbreakingly difficult. Mike had solved that problem in his second year, but had never been able to turn it off. The alien rec room had to be kept in vacuo, with a separate airlock, because air disappeared into the little ball of nothing at the end of the sculpting tool.

Enough progress had been made on the alien number system that it was possible to do calculus with it. The money system, however, remained a complete mystery.

Aside from the crystal maker and the airlock controls, the ship was as great and as fascinating an enigma as ever. The rows of "bunks" near the back—suppose a bunk changed shape and dumped its occupant during a 5G maneuver? The controls, in plain sight on a common-sense control board in the bunk section—what did it take to make them work? And what was the purpose of the dull red tetrahedron, seven feet on a side, which was set in the rear wall of the passenger section?

Mike was taking a coffee break with Terry Holmes, a pretty, cheerful, blonde little Doctor of Languages, the day he first said, "I think I know what the central pyramid is for."

Many people had said that, of course, but Mike was not addicted to wild guesses. "What is it?" Terry asked eagerly.

"It's a time machine," he said.

Terry got mad and left the table. The Halloween before Mike had dressed to imitate an alien statue and had frighteningly "come to life" before her horrified eyes. Since then she had been sensitive about his jokes.

"No, really," he told her during the afternoon coffee break. "The idea makes a great deal of sense. We can be sure that the aliens had suspended animation, can't we?"

"Sure." The reaction damping field was perfect for that purpose.

"Right. So if they had time travel to go with it, it adds up to an FTL drive. They can sleep through a hundred-year journey and then move back a hundred years."

"You're only guessing," Terry told him. "If the pyramid is an interstellar drive they didn't need time travel. If they had suspended animation they could have spent generations on one trip. We'll have to do that ourselves, probably."

"Sure, but the idea of a time-travel device in the center of a spaceship is at least logical. I've been working on the thing for quite a while, and I think that's what it is. I've made it produce a weak gravitational field, so I know it can distort four-space."

"Then it's for artificial gravity." She laughed as his face fell. "Mike, I dub thee world's champion rationalizer. And now I've got to get back to work."

For a month nothing important happened. Carlos found a way to turn on the alien television set and got three-dimensional, technicolor static. Terry made some progress with the alien money; she had a tentative ordering of coins into either ascending or descending value, if in fact they were coins.

Then one day the ship disappeared.

Mike was trying something new. He had set up a magnetic field around the control board and pushed one of the pyramid knobs. There were two of these, the same shape and color as the massive machine behind him. Now he put a block of glass between the poles of his generator and cut the current. The knob lit with an almost invisible blue glow. Suddenly everything was in free fall.

"Eureka," Mike said absently, meaning: at last I've gotten some action out of the beast. When he turned his head he saw that the big red tetrahedron was base forward. He'd heard no sound of motion.

A faint purple line grew across the top of the board.

There were too many unknowns crawling into his experiment. Mike looked back so that he could see the big pyramid turn around, and switched his generator back on. Results came instantly.

Mike sat up trying to rub the pain out of his eyes. It was several seconds before he could open them.

The pyramid was apex-forward again. Mike got up and pulled out the pyramid knob, waited a moment for luck, then turned off the field generator. At last he sat down perspiring on an alien "bunk." What a sight that had been! He couldn't even remember it without his eyes hurting.

Mike's bunk inconsiderately dropped him on the floor. He promptly got up and made for the airlock, feeling a crying need for coffee, Terry Holmes, conversation and familiar things. The strangeness had suddenly become too much to take.

His momentary fear of the ship was gone by the time he left the airlock. What had started it, anyway? Merely the fact that he'd gotten things to working at last. Now they could make some real progress.

He moved toward the base in easy four-foot leaping strides which splashed waves of dust when he landed. He was looking straight at the base airlock, but he was preoccupied by the thought of coffee and the familiar, instantly suppressed wish for a cigarette. He was half way there before he noticed . . .

The base airlock was closed. The *alien* airlock!

Mike stopped short, staring. At first he was only bewildered, not horrified. How could the doors have closed? The bulk of the UN airlock would have stopped them. Or was the alien metal strong enough to—

Mike made a strangling noise. The human airlock must have been crushed flat!

He ran.

It had taken the base team months to open those doors. Although Mike had arrived a year later, he knew how they had done it. But why had they closed it? Had some fool been meddling with the controls?

With alien designing, practically anything could be a control. The aliens had cleverly hidden their knobs, buttons, and pressure sensitive surfaces in æsthetically pleasing design. The doors could have been closed by somebody accidentally leaning against a wall. Nobody had ever bothered to find out how to open them from the inside.

Mike began picking pressure points out of the mosaic on the outer door. He stopped to wonder if the base held air, then decided that it didn't matter. Anyone still alive would be wearing a spacesuit under emergency regulations.

He was taking a breather when he noticed that the UN ship was gone.

Had they started to evacuate the base? No, the ship only held four people and cargo. They must have gone for help.

The lock had been designed for use by two ten-footers with fourteen-foot branched tentacles. Mike needed forty minutes and a great deal of ingenuity, but finally the lock swung open.

There was no wreckage in the lock.

"Dust," Mike told himself. There was almost no moondust on the worn path between the ship and the base. Yet dust had spurted beneath his boots . . . and there was no Earth-built ship, and the station was locked.

"Eureka," he said softly. "They haven't found the base yet. I've traveled in time."

Yet there were other possibilities. Mike began seeking them out even as he was going to work on the inner door. Maybe he had gone forward in time, to when the base had been restored as a museum. Or, worse yet, to some time after the return of the legitimate owners. (That had once been a favorite joke around the base: "Hey, look, they're coming back!") He might even be in another time track, one in which the base had never been abandoned. After all, he really didn't know much about the machine he'd been running.

One look through a telescope would have told all. He could see the Earth from where he was standing, huge and full, of course, he could not make out the shapes of the continents.

He kept working.

He was rigidly tensed as the doors folded back. Had the station been abandoned yet? Was his the honor, God help him, of meeting the first inhuman intelligence? But nobody came to meet him.

His air pressure dial read 22.4 pounds/square inch. This must be alien air.

He walked through the base, slowly and cautiously; after four and a half years he was used to watching where he stepped. The base was like a haunted house. There was an air of strangeness here that he had never known before, not even when he had first come. Not Commander Link Day of UN Flight Four, but Mike Capoferri, was the first man to set foot in this place.

Could he get back? Sure he could. The other button must be the one that controlled flight into the future.

But even then, he might not be able to tell anyone. *Hey,* he told himself proudly, *I'm a time traveler! Wait here,* he answered solicitously, *I'll call the medic. No,* he protested, *I can prove it. Get in the ship and I'll show you.* But that could go wrong in a dozen ways. He'd want to know more about what he was doing before he tried this again.

Kilroy was here, he thought.

If he left marks of his visit, they would still be here when he returned to his own time. He could scratch his initials—hmm.

He turned right. When he reached the rec room he went to one of the sculpting machines and began to take it apart.

The tool itself looked like a big, fat mechanical pencil. It was set in a brace which could be moved to any part of the work. The brace allowed the tool to move freely under pressure and held it steady otherwise. The pointed business end of the tool generated a sphere of emptiness into which matter vanished without trace.

Removing the tool from the brace was almost easy. Turning it on took just under an hour. Once Mike almost gave up the idea, but he kept at it, for he had nothing else which would mar any of the indestructible materials used to build the base.

He held the device like a pencil, but more carefully. His first thought had been to put a portrait of Commander Link Day on the statue of an alien female in the bunk room. He'd changed his mind. It would be dangerous and stupid to change his own past. He had to do something which would not be discovered before he arrived at the base, in 1985.

The inner side of the outer door would be a good place to hide a carving, because nobody had ever seen it. It folded against the airlock wall when the lock was open.

A wind blew toward his hand as he walked. There must be a way to shut air out of the disintegrator, but he hadn't the time to find it. He couldn't remember whether the team had found air in the base. If they had, he was changing the past right now.

What should he write? "The world is my ash tray," he decided, and slammed his toe into a ledge. He threw both hands out to break his fall, and changed his mind too late. Horrified, he watched the sculpting pencil vanish into the floor. It left a neat cylindrical hole.

Well, Mike thought furiously, that takes care of that. I've made my mark.

He plugged the hole with cement from the meteor repair kit on his suit belt. There was now a machine missing from the base, one that had been there in his own time, but he couldn't do anything about that. He did manage to close the airlock doors as he left.

The breathtaking beauty of the full Earth stopped him outside the ship. He gazed at the magnificent bluish-white disk, trying to decide what made it seem different. Was there more cloud area? Whatever the reason, the sight was more impressive than ever.

Then it came to him. The Earth was bigger! It was probably twice as large as he had ever seen it. Of course, there was nothing nearby to compare it to, which was why he hadn't noticed before.

Mike was smiling as he entered the lock. The Moon has been moving outward from the Earth since creation, picking up energy from the slowing of the Earth's rotation. He must be a long way into the past. About three billion years . . .

He pushed through the inner door and stood a moment, looking down the three broken rows—one along the floor of the ship, the others down the sides—of amethyst portholes. It would have been nice to be able to see out, but the glassy material was transparent only to a wide range of ultraviolet light.

He went through the motions at the control panel. Right pyramid knob in—and it had better be the right move. Generator on. Glass block between the poles. Generator off.

He floated.

Suddenly, remembering the sight of the central pyramid "turning," Mike was glad that he could not see the ship traveling through time. Obviously the aliens could stand the sight—but they could also look at the central pyramid, for they had done nothing to protect themselves from it.

A green line crept across the board, covering and wiping out the faint purple line. Mike let it grow until the purple line was gone, then slipped on his generator.

Wrong, Wrong! He was still in free fall!

In hideous indecision he watched the board, waiting for it to tell him—it didn't matter what, for the board was quiet and dark. In the end he left the knob in and the generator on and pushed himself aft. He had to get a look outside.

He braced himself in the airlock, suspiciously examining the brilliant sky for any sign that he was still traveling in time. There was nothing. Mike turned on his shoes and gingerly stepped out onto the hull. When he looked down, the Moon wasn't there.

A misty white planet floated nearby. It was a heavy atmosphere type, as uniform and featureless as a piece of bedsheet. It was Venus, if he was still in the solar system. Otherwise—heavy atmospheres are the norm in space.

It seemed obvious now that he'd guessed wrong. The knob on the left must control time travel; the one on the right, space travel. It was a chance he'd had to take.

Mike watched the white disk slowly setting toward one horizon of the ship. As the last thing he might see in life, it left a lot to be desired. Still, blank as it was, he could tell quite a bit about it. It couldn't be very large, for instance. If it were a giant, its atmosphere would be banded. It must be bigger than Mars to have an opaque atmosphere, but, unless an oversized moon had stripped away most of the air, it couldn't be much larger than Earth.

When he saw its star he could try guessing its surface temperature.

He sat down on the hull. There were two days' worth of oxygen in the ship, and little chance that it would get him home. He was lost in both space and time. He didn't know how to go into the future; if there was a way, he could expect to spend months looking for it. It was time to face death.

Besides, he'd been running for hours, torn by conflicting emotions, through a world whose laws were more black magic than physics. It was high time for a coffee break.

Mike licked dry lips. That last, lost cup of coffee would have tasted wonderful. A cigarette would have torn his throat out after four and a half years, but it would have felt natural and smelled good smoldering between his fingers.

He'd left precious little legacy for the others at the base, a spare spacesuit that couldn't fit anyone else, three sets of lounging overalls, and a few interesting discoveries. He'd taken the spaceship; they'd cuss him out good for that . . .

Or had he ever lived at all? He had died before he was born. Perhaps there would be no Mike Capoferri, ever.

But UN Flight Four would find his anonymous traces when they opened the base. Footprints in moon-dust. A sculpting tool missing from the rec room. A hole in the floor; his cement was sure to disintegrate in three billion years. Would they ever guess how deep it was? The damn thing must have fallen all the way to the center of the Moon.

Searing light stabbed his eyes. Mike groped blindly for his filter switch, and found it. The light became bearable.

A sun was rising over the hull. It looked very much like the Sun as seen from the Moon; but that only meant that it wasn't. Seen from a Venus orbit, the Sun would have been much larger. He was in another solar system.

Could the ship have come home by itself? Was that the home world of the base race? No, of course not. The aliens had had a water metabolism, and there would be no water down there. That world, in an Earth-like orbit around a type G yellow dwarf, must have a surface temperature of around five hundred degrees Fahrenheit.

Mr. Parkman in Physics 1B had told the class one day that "The Earth's atmosphere goes 'way past the Moon." He seemed surprised by their laughter. It was his highly successful way of holding their attention. "No, it's true. Of course, it gets pretty thin. The idea is that the Earth's atmosphere ends where its density drops to the density of surrounding space. In the same way the Sun's atmosphere goes out beyond Mars.

"Well, the air is thin enough to behave like separate particles at that distance. So the Moon is constantly whipping through this cloud of gas molecules"—he made frantic motions with his hands—"and it pulls some of them up to escape velocity every time it goes by. Naturally they're never heard from again. The air keeps replacing itself, more or less, by volcanic action. '

"Now, most planets don't have giant moons, so they grow tremendous air envelopes. Like Venus. Here's where the greenhouse effect comes in . . ."

Mike snapped back to the present because of something small and dark and spinning. With the light filter over his eyes he couldn't see more. 'He looked away. Something was worrying at the bottom of his mind.

Again his mind's eye watched the sculpting tool fall into a tunnel of its own making. He saw it lying at the center of the Moon, perhaps carving out a little pit for itself . . .

Wrong. There would be millions of tons of pressure to flatten any cavity into oblivion . . .

Any cavity but one. Now the picture was right.

The Sun had dropped below the hull, though part of the corona still showed. Mike raised his filter and searched for the spinning blob. He knew what it was, now.

At first glance it looked like a walnut shell; but not quite, for the shape was wrong and the convolutions were too deep. What it really resembled was a deflated beach ball which somebody has crushed between his hands.

The Moon had had a long time to push itself through a sphere an inch and a half in diameter. Probably it had not taken more than a few millennia. Afterward there had been nothing but this crumpled ball of waste, too light and rigid for gravity to compress it further. For three billion years the Earth had been moonless.

". . . Six to eight hundred degrees!" Mr. Parkman waited a moment while the scribblers caught up. "They knew about the greenhouse effect, but they hadn't dreamed that it would apply to little Venus. You could melt lead in such a greenhouse!

"The point is, the astronomers were using Earth as a norm. It isn't. The Earth-Moon system is an astronomical freak. A normal planet in Earth's orbit would have an opaque, very thick atmosphere, so thick that wind and light and temperature changes would never reach the surface. An eternal searing black calm."

Mike turned and crawled into the airlock, moving as fast as he dared in free fall. He could have gone mad waiting for the inner door to open, but he didn't dare. The knowledge of certain death had been better than this aching sense of responsibility.

The door opened and he jumped toward the control board. Already he was planning. He had to go back some time before his first arrival. Then—remove the sculpting tools from the rec room, or somehow scramble the controls of the base airlock, or leave a message for "himself" on the outer door. Anything to restore the past.

The glass block had not floated out of place. All he had to do was cut the magnetic field. He watched the purple line until he was sure that it was longer than it had been before. When he flipped the generator back on his feet thumped satisfyingly against the floor. Half the battle.

Ghosts from his childhood whispered to him while he waited for the outer door to open. Parkman was there but Mike refused to listen to him. He remembered Tony; which was unfair, because he'd only robbed Tony of eight years.

The door opened on the Moon. Mike bounded toward the base . . . Or had he? He really should have known better than to loan Tony his Flexy. His Flexy, because Tony's had a broken wheel. Had he told Doctor Stuart that? No.

"Time is a one-way street," said Doctor Stuart, sympathetically but firmly. He was wrong, dead wrong.

Mike stood before the base airlock wriggling his fingers like a clarinet player. How far back had he come this time? He turned left to see the size of the Earth.

It wasn't there.

But it was always there! Bewildered, Mike peered around him. The Moon must still be rotating . . .

To his right, the Earth was a vast, incredible crescent —and the plain was full of ships. They were of many different sizes, but they all had the same lumpy cylindrical shape. Tiny figures moved among them.

Stuart was right, he thought idiotically. You go the wrong way on a one-way street, you've got to have accidents. He turned and ran.

Behind him the lock swung open. Two ten-foot tripeds turned to each other and gestured rapidly, like nests of striking snakes. Then one of them hopped after him and picked him up.